1

I took two paces back. Then two more.

'Well, what can you see in the painting, what does it say to you.'

I stared at the canvas. And was aware of a group of schoolchildren staring at me, some giggling and pointing, until their teacher moved them on. And I really did concentrate. Staring hard at the canvas on the white painted wall with its hue of blood red paint screaming loudly. Thing is though, however hard it screamed at me I was just not getting it. Abstract and modern art in general was not my thing. Not my cup of tea. Piles of bricks, driftwood artly arranged and all that conceptual stuff left me cold. Now and again I may find something interesting, but only now and again. In the main I found the vast majority of it pretentious and vacuous, over-intellectualised, shallow rubbish, and not my words, something that I read and agreed with. The canvas was a big splash of red paint and that was about it. For me at least. But not for her.

'It must be saying something, surely. Take a good hard look. A frenetic daubing of red and totally awesome. But why the grey area, the small grey area in the corner of the canvas. It must represent something. What is it saying to you. Say something. Fuck. Anything. That is what it is all about. To challenge you, to make something of it. Have a go, if only to please me.'

Right then. But I had nothing to say. Clueless. It was just a swirling sea of red and a patch of grey and could mean anything. Literally any old thing. So she gave up. She shook her head and sighed. I was a dummy.

'The canvas is by the Albanian artist Zuber Shala. It was only discovered after his death. Killed while fighting in the bloody conflict in Kosovo. Untitled it is his last known piece of work. I see pain and suffering with every layer of paint that he puts onto that canvas, you can see that he has applied it with a pallet knife, brushes and also used his hands to spread the paint over the canvas. First he has applied a layer of grey paint then overpainted with the red but leaving a corner untouched. The canvas just seems so deeply personal like he had really put his heart and soul into it, pouring every emotion into what would be his last piece of work. That is what it says to me.'

I could only see a sea of mad red paint. My brain hurts. So I held my head in my hands and pulled a face, mimicking the work by the artist, Edvard Munch. The Scream. And she laughed and did the same back. Then grabbed my arm and held on tight as we slowly made our way past the people paying homage to the brightly hung paintings and other works on show. And I could not help my philistine feelings that a bunch of chimps let loose with paint brushes and gallons of paint could turn out work of equal merit. And that made me smile just thinking about it. They weren't gonna make a monkey of me with their witless words on the artwork on show.

Back outside in the sunshine and I fancied a beer so I eyed up a nice pub a short walk away. 'Fancy a beer,' I said as we made for the pub with seating outside, that was beckoning me. She pulled a face. 'Come on, one drink won't kill you. Have half a Guinness. Guinness is good for you.'

'Okay, but no alcohol for me. Hard as it is, I plan to stick to it. But once this baby is out. Boy will I have a good drink.'

'Too right,' I said, smiling back at her. So. Heavily pregnant with our first child she slowly walked alongside to a table and I pulled out a chair for her to sit on while I got a beer and a bottle of water. She collapsed onto the chair, so glad to take the weight off her feet, the utter relief showing in her face.

She sat and watched him go into the pub for their drinks and stroked her swollen belly. Not long to go and she can feel normal again. She had a backache. Her legs ached. Her breasts felt heavy and swollen, two milk sacks for the waiting baby to feed on, months of breast-feeding before she could get them back. Before he could get them back. He had lost all interest in sex in the later part of her pregnancy and it worried her, though she could hardly blame him for his lack of desire. She had a big fat belly and why would he want to hump a whale. Amazingly though, he showered her with compliments. Her skin was soft as peach, her hair thick and lustrous. She glowed with health and looked beautiful, so he said. But once the baby is born, as friends had warned, her skin will look shit through tiredness, her hair will lose its lustre and as for sex, forget it. All she will want to do is sleep.

I put the drinks on the table and sat down. Looked at her. She looked kind of anxious. 'Penny for your thoughts,' I said.

'They are mine and a penny won't buy them,' she said back. And smiled to reassure me things were fine.

I picked up my pint and took a mouthful and it felt wonderful, nothing like a pulled pint of beer outside on a warm day. But I made sure that my face didn't show too much pleasure as she was looking at me and very jealous of my beer while she stuck to water. Then I took to thinking about the baby with the birth now looming large. Boy or girl and it didn't matter as long as it was healthy. And the birth goes okay, no drama when it happens.

A pair of mounted police clipped-clopped past. One of the horses, a dark bay gelding, raised its tail and did a shit and I was glad of the distraction from worrying about the baby and the birth.

'Do my feet,' she suddenly said. 'My dogs are barking. Killing me they are. Be a sweetheart.' And a pump landed in my lap. I pulled off the pump and obliged. Massaging her foot. Then gently massaged her little pigs as she squealed with delight. I could see the bliss in her beautiful face.

'That is heaven. Do the other one.'

So I did. 'Guess who is in the pub. Jason Statham and Jason Flemying.'

'I suppose you said hello.'

'Yeah. I did. And we did a selfie,' and I got out my phone and brought up the picture of me and the two film stars smiling for the camera and showed it to her.

She smiled. 'The three Js.'

I smiled back. Was pleased. Loved, Lock Stock and Snatch. A slice of life that I would never see. A gun pushed in your face, all that violence, nor Jason Statham or Jason Flemying for that matter, sat in the pub having a quiet drink together and pretty much left alone. And I finished her feet and finished the beer. Phoned for a cab. She was looking at a little girl feeding some pigeons from her packet of crisps in what was becoming a feeding frenzy. The grey mass grew as they fought for the crisps cooing and flapping while the little girl giggled out loud. The little girl was adorable, a real poppet.

'Hope our little girl is as cute as her, if it is a girl that is,' she said, laughing at the little girl as she flapped her arms along with the pigeons, pretending that she was a pigeon.

'If we have a girl and she is half as gorgeous as her mother, I will be the happiest man alive.' I really meant it as I gazed at her, I really did.

She squeezed my hand and kissed me, just as the black cab that I had ordered pulled up. I helped her in and she was asleep in moments, her face dreamy, her hands resting on her magnificent mound.

I went into the bedroom. She came out from the en-suite bathroom after a long soak in the bath. She was holding a bottle of Bio-Oil oil ready to oil her stomach in her hope to avoid stretch marks, and wearing nothing but a smile.

'I'll do that.' I took the bottle from her while she made herself comfortable.

'Lovely being pampered, feel like the Queen of Sheba,' she said, laying back naked on the bed.

I squirted the Bio-Oil onto her stomach before putting the bottle down. Then slowly worked the oil all over with my outstretched fingers, gently, mindful of our baby inside. I traced around her large belly button. 'Feels strange,' I said. Staring at her swollen stomach.

'What does. My belly button,' she said, pulling a face.

'No. Us. You know, having a baby. This baby is growing inside of you and it feels, dunno, weird. No …' I said, looking at her face as she frowned. Weird was wrong. 'Not weird, obviously. Overwhelming, I guess. But in a wonderful way. And I can't wait till it is born, I really can't. Never been more excited about anything, and never more happy.' I had a beautiful wife and now a baby to look forward to. I felt blessed.

'Me too. Never been happier, and can't wait, really can't wait till the baby is born. They say the last bit is the hardest and they have that right. Can't wait to get back to normal, get my body back, touch my toes … and other things …'

And she looked at me as she said, and other things. So I kind of ignored it, looked down at her stomach, away from her gaze, and her eyes, that were sexual and sad at the same time. Carried on massaging the oil into her soft skin and changed the subject.

'Still haven't got a name yet, can't call it Bumpy-Lumpy forever. Maybe we'll look at it and a name will just fit. Still like Alfred. Alfred Ramsey, 1966 and the World Cup win. I do like Alfred …' and my fingers were drifting towards her pubic mound, so I pulled them back.

'Do my breasts,' she said. Pushing her arms above her head and exposing her two breasts, plump and inviting.

So I did. Gently massaging the oil around the nipples, as they slowly erected.

'Do you want to,' she said, staring at me. Willing me. 'You can you know. As long as we're careful, take it slow. From behind. I'd like that.'

I stopped massaging her breasts. I kind of felt bad.

'Do I take that as no,' as she read my silence.

I looked at her sad face, the tears forming in her eyes. I felt really bad. Of course I wanted to. She was gorgeous and incredibly sexy.

'What is wrong. It's me, isn't it. I am fat, a fat fucking whale. A big fat fucking walrus. Fuck me in this state, who am I fucking kidding. You don't fancy me one bit …' and the tears flowed.

'Of course I still fancy you. Really fucking fancy you. You don't know how hard it is.'

'But.'

My face was easy to read. 'Okay. It's the baby. It is that simple. Puts me off, and it kind of doesn't feel right. It's there isn't it, you can see its outline, see it moving.'

She wiped the tears from her face. Sniffed. 'What about a blowjob.'

I looked at her mouth, her sensual lips, and was quite tempted. But the baby would still be there between us. 'When this baby is out. We can make love again.'

'I will hold you to that.'

2

'Who was that,' she asked as I came back into the house.

'Delivery guy.'

'Delivering what.'

'Paint.'

'Paint for what.'

This could have gone on all day. 'For the garage. We had talked about it, the new concrete floor was only sealed by the builder and that will wear away, I guess. So I ordered garage floor paint. Thought I'd get on and do it. It makes sense.'

'Can't you get the builder back to do it.'

'Painting the garage floor will give me something to do. It needs doing. And I don't mind doing it.' She smiled. Which is good.

'Okay. It does need doing.'

'Gonna get changed, put on an old tracksuit bottom and t-shirt.'

I was at home because the baby was imminent. And I wanted to be at the birth so was given leave of absence.

'Want a cup of tea before you start. Mum is coming round, so I'll be making tea.'

She was an angel, a very beautiful angel. 'That would be lovely.'

Her mum was also an angel, a kind of older version of her daughter, and we got on well, and I was glad. Lovely to have a lovely mother-in-law, rather than the myth of the old dragon. Wyn was welcome anytime. So I had a cup of tea before starting, and then left them to it.

'A granny soon. Imagine that, a granny. Wonder what I will be, granny, grandma, grandmother. All make you sound old. I remember looking at my grandparents and they seemed so bloody ancient, all wrinkly. Wise and wrinkly, that will be me. Grandmother seems formal, grandma too old somehow. Maybe just granny. Oh I don't know, where did it all go, one minute I have a baby in my arms and the next my baby is all grown up and having a baby of her own. Anyway. Back to you, you look in good health, and the baby is too.'

'Yes, mum. Had a check-up the other day and all is good to go, and frankly I can't wait.'

'Bet you can't. I couldn't wait to get you out,' and Wyn laughed along with her daughter.

'Anyway, do you like my necklace. Lovely, isn't it. The daughter of a family from Eritrea made it for me. It is gorgeous, I was really touched.'

Wyn was a volunteer at a refuge centre and very passionate about her work there helping the refugees as they navigated the asylum system. She was an activist. Not an anarchist. Definitely not an anarchist. Wyn would never be seen in a black beret, stab vest and army fatigue pants with a raised angry fist. She was a gentle soul, and liked to get involved just to make the world, in her eyes, a better place. She did not even see it as activism, more just caring for others.

Wyn pushed the plate of biscuits towards her daughter. And smiled as they were pushed back.

'No thanks, mum. Though I could. Easily. Eat the whole packet no trouble, but I have to stop myself. All that eating for two is bollocks, you just end up fat. Fat and miserable is not for me. Can't wait to lose some of this weight, honestly, mum, I just feel sluggish. Just not me.'

Wyn stood up and started to clear up. Washing the cups and saucers before putting them on the draining board. Sat back down with her daughter.

I came to a halt. Run out of paint. Could you believe it, fuck sake. Just a small area of grey concrete left. Bollocks. I thought, well kind of knew, based on the advice given, that two cans would be enough for the area that I needed to paint. It was a big area, a big garage for several cars and all the other stuff. Our bikes, you name it. What people fill a garage with. Bollocks. I would have to get some more and knew I couldn't leave it. I came out into the sunshine from the open garage doors, put my can and brush down and stretched myself out. Boy, did that feel good after being on my knees hunched over a paint can painting away for the past, dunno, seemed like hours. I looked for my phone to check the time. But remembered that I had left it in the house on charge. I stretched out again, pushing my arms out as far as they would go. I was a newly emerged butterfly shaking out my wings in the summer sunshine. I felt great as the aches just melted away, warmed from the overhead sun.

'Have you finished it.'

They both looked at me. Looked me up and down, looking at my once white t-shirt stained with red paint where I had wiped my hands on it. My tracksuit bottoms with red knees after kneeling in the paint once too often. I looked a bit of a mess, a bloody mess. Literally.

'God, you look like you've been in a knife fight, or shot or something. All that red paint.'

I pulled a face. 'And it's not finished.'

They looked in the garage, the small area of grey concrete that was still to do. They laughed.

'If you had not got so much paint on yourself, then maybe there would have been enough to finish it,' said Wyn. Helpfully.

'Well I do want to finish it today. So I'm going to get some more paint, enough to finish that last bit. Going to walk there. A walk there and back will do me the world of good. I've been on my knees bent over for the last hour or so.'

'You sure.'

'Quite sure.' And I was. I really needed to stretch my legs and the walk in the sunshine would do me the power of good.

She put her hands on her stomach. 'Hurry though, don't want you gone too long. The baby won't wait, you know.'

'I promise. Won't be long.'

'Have you got any money, you know, for the paint that you intend to buy.'

'Um. No.'

'Card or cash.'

'Card if you go and get my card from my wallet. Or cash. What's ever easier.'

3

'How did it go.'

'Not very well. She said no, you can keep it. I am not paying any money to get him back.'

'You offered her a deal, come down, at least we get something for our troubles.'

'Yeah I did. But she still said no. I said okay then, I will fucking shoot it. Have that on your conscience, eh.'

'You are not shooting it …' and he held on tight to the Yorkshire Terrier sitting on his lap.

He dropped the two fingers that he had made into a gun, while pulling a sour face. 'Okay. I won't shoot it. But we're not keeping it. Yappy little thing.' He picked up his mug of tea and finished it, putting the empty mug back on the table. Wiped his mouth.

He got an angry face in response. 'I'll keep it. We can't sell it and I'm not dumping it, and she doesn't deserve it back.'

'Okay. Okay. Keep the fucking thing, but you look after it.' He put a cigarette in his mouth taken from a packet on the table. Lit it.

'So now what. I am getting tired of this. Stealing dogs.'

'It's good money, when they pay up that is. But I agree. It won't get that parcel of land that you always talk about. And to build your own house. That you have set your heart on. And it won't get me …' he sighed. He wanted to buy a boat and sail away to the sun. Have the money to do that. His dream.

As a kid he would holiday every summer on the Isle of Wight with his uncle. His uncle lived for boats. Owned a beautiful boat and would take him out sailing. Taught him to sail. His uncle said that he was a natural, as he picked it up quickly, till he was able to take full control of the boat as they sailed around the Island. Spending days and nights away at sea just the two of them. It was as far away from his home in Canning Town in East London as you could get. Then home in London he got the news. His uncle had been attacked in a local pub by a gang of youths. Left hospitalised fighting for his life. Wouldn't take to the sea again after his injuries, and died two years after the attack. The youths all escaped jail. Laughed in court. Laughed outside of court. Said his uncle had started it and that they were only defending themselves. The police couldn't make a case of it, so they walked free.

He got a ferry over to the Isle of Wight. And found out where the youths hung out. Threatened them with a loaded shotgun that he had acquired from someone in Ryde. A stolen shotgun. He was arrested and dealt with by the Youth Justice System. Sent to a Young Offenders Institution for two years. Released at 18. Jobless. Homeless. He never knew his dad and his mum had died of cancer while he was serving his sentence. A young man with a criminal record, jobs were hard to come by. An angry young man with a gun in his hand, who had lost the two people that he most cared about, cared little about anyone now.

He picked up a newspaper from the table and turned to the back pages and the football. He pulled hard on his cigarette and blew the smoke slowly out, while he read the newspaper. More stories about Jack Jones, the gifted young player that had it all. The world at his feet. Every major club was after him and he could be sold for a record fee. He closed his eyes. Alone on his boat he sailed the seven seas. He opened his eyes. 'I think I have an idea.'

4

Days later they sat in the parked van on a quiet street and looked across at the imposing Edwardian Villa set back behind a high wall, its frontage covered in wisteria.

'So this is your big idea. And now I can see it is no more than that, an idea. Not reality. See for yourself the reality. The property has a high wall and large gates with security cameras. We will never break into that. He will come out in one of his cars. It will be very hard to try and stop him and get him out of his car I would say. Very hard. Okay not impossible. But hard all the same.'

'Think positive. The bigger the risk the bigger the reward. Granted. It may be a stretch to break in … but when he comes out in one of his cars we can follow and carjack him. Out of the car that he is in and into the back of the van.'

'You make it sound so easy.'

'No it won't be that easy. A million things could go wrong. But if we want to make some serious money for once. Enough money to change our lives and to capture our dreams. Sail off into the sunset. Buy yourself that plot of land that you've always wanted. Build your dream home. We have to at least give it a go. And no different than taking dogs, right. Taking him will just pay better. A lot better.'

'I still think it is risky. If your boat leaks like this plan does you'll never make it out of port. We are looking at the house. Very high security, yes. And carjacking … I am not convinced of that.'

He sighed. 'Look. Do I have to paint you a picture. I am solo sailing from California to Hawaii. The Caribbean, the Windward Islands and the Leeward Islands. I drop anchor and swim in crystal clear water, beaches of fine white sand. I go ashore and spend time with the locals, I want to taste paradise. Meantime. You have your land that you've always dreamt about. Acres and acres to plant your vines and make your own wine. Build your house brick by brick to your own specifications, using the best craftsmen that money can buy. You sip your wine that you have produced on your piece of heaven on earth, on the veranda of your dream home as the sun sets. And you are at peace. We both are.'

And as he spoke the gates suddenly opened and out stepped Jack Jones …

The sun was overhead and felt warm on my face. It would be a pleasant walk into town … until a van pulled up. A guy jumped out from the passenger side. And he was waving a gun. A fucking gun in broad daylight. Shouting at me, get in the van, get in the fucking van, with the barrel of the gun inches from my face. I really didn't have time to react. It was all so quick. Even if I had shouted out for help it would have done me no good, there was not a soul about. And it may have got me killed if the guy with the gun panicked. This wasn't robbery, I was being forcibly kidnapped at gunpoint. And you can't argue with a gun in your face. Take a chance on the gun being real or fake. A toy gun that would bang a lot of caps in my face. Or a real gun that would leave a bullet hole. Anyway all this happening was a blur, over in seconds. Only later would you go over the events in your head. The guy with a gun in my face grabbed me and the next thing I was in the back of the van face down with him straddling me and the gun sticking in the back of my neck.

5

'Mum… Jack isn't back yet … he has been gone for too long. He didn't take his phone. I found it on charge. Mum, mum, I think it's started …'

'Are you okay …'

'Mum … mum … I think I'm in labour …'

6

'Push, push, push, that's it, push, my darling. You are doing so well … keep it up, keep pushing. That's it, my love, push. You are so nearly there, just one hard push …'

And the baby emerges and is swiftly out, and into safe hands. Then an anxious moment while the mouth is cleared of fluid and to hear the baby utter its first cry. Then it does and it has a nice set of lungs. And it is beautiful.

'It's a girl. A beautiful baby girl. Oh my darling, it's gorgeous beyond words. A beautiful baby girl …'

The beautiful baby girl is placed in the grateful arms of its mother, who is spent, and her emotions all at sea. And she looked at her mum, and she loved her mum dearly. But it should have been Jack holding her hand and giving her words of encouragement. Looking on proudly at their beautiful baby daughter. And she looked at her precious daughter and wept.

7

The van had pulled to a stop. The gunman got off of me and sat on the floor of the van holding his gun. We seemed to stop for quite a while before moving again. I could hear the sound of traffic as the van made its way, slowing down, starting and stopping, crawling through the traffic of London. Then it seemed to make progress wherever that they were heading for. The van slowed down as we made a turn. We were now on an unmade road, face down on the metal floor of the van I could feel every pothole that the van went over. And the van stopped and I could feel myself sweating, feeling nauseous after being on the floor of the van for so long. And wasn't sure that this was the final destination. I knew that I had to try and remain calm, I didn't want to get killed. I had to be brave, I guess, and face up to the situation that I had been kidnapped. Not do anything stupid that could get me killed. The van doors were opened and whoever opened them threw a plastic carrier bag inside. The gunman grabbed the plastic carrier bag.

'Put this over your head.'

I had to get up on my knees while I did this. I guess that they didn't want me to see where they had taken me to. And the dark coloured carrier bag made sure of that.

'Now get out.'

Getting out of the van was awkward to say the least, stooping in the van while I stood up, then feeling my way before gingerly putting a foot out. But grabbed by whoever was outside the van before I took a tumble. Which I did anyway and fell onto the ground. I went to get up and pulled the carrier bag back right over my head, so as to not make them angry. Once back on my feet I was manhandled roughly with a tight grip on my arm twenty or so paces before I was stopped.

I could hear a key being put into a lock, and then the door being opened. And then I was pushed in. I am thinking. Unmade road. This was somewhere out of the way, had to be. But the sound of traffic before we turned onto the unmade road meant it could not be in the middle of nowhere. I had the feeling that we had not gone that far out of London.

'Move.'

I was pushed in the back. Made my way slowly, like a blind man with my hands out in front feeling my way. I came to a staircase.

'Up.'

I held onto the bannister and made my way up the stairs till I got to the landing. I stood there while one of them got past me and opened a door.

'In.'

I was pushed into the room.

'Sit on the floor.'

I did as told and sat on the floor with my legs out in front. Then unexpectedly and without warning, the plastic carrier bag was pulled from my head. And the gunman stood over me.

'Sit tight and don't make any trouble for yourself. Keep your trap closed and just do as you are asked. You do that and everything will work out fine. Don't even think about escaping. Don't think for a moment that I wouldn't hesitate to shoot you if you play up.'

He pointed the handgun at me like he meant it. His eyes had a glint, sinister I would say, hard and cold. He dropped his hand with the gun.

'Gonna go now, bud. One of us will be back later with some food for you. This ain't the Ritz Hotel so don't expect anything fancy. And you must be thirsty as well after your trip. A nice cup of tea would go down well, eh.'

And he left the room. Closed the door and locked it with a turn of the key. And once he had gone I lay stretched out on the floor. And for some reason, and I don't know why, I was sound asleep, out like a light.

I woke up, rubbed my eyes, yawned. Looked around. And guess what. It wasn't the Ritz Hotel. It was a room with bare floorboards, faded painted walls and woodwork, and was airless and musty. The only furniture is a stickback chair. A small window up high with bars on, and little chance of escaping from. And a rolled up sleeping mat and sleeping bag. Brand new and with price tags attached. And they definitely were not there when I first came into the room, I am sure that I would have noticed them. Neither was the pack of toilet rolls. And a folded towel. And a plastic carrier bag alongside. I went to the carrier bag and opened it out to look inside. Then took out what was in it. A toothbrush and toothpaste. Bar of soap and a flannel. A supermarket sandwich and a small bottle of water. Suddenly I was hungry and grateful for the food and drink. So I ate the sandwich and drank the water. Feeling better for it. Used the carrier bag as a rubbish bag after. I again looked at the sleeping bag and sleeping mat. Comfort, I thought. They are making me comfortable, if they were going to kill me why go to the bother. I had to think positive, glass half full, which was my nature anyway. Was a sunny sort of guy, so I was told by most people that I knew. Then I thought, how did I sleep through it all. The comings and goings while the things were put in the room. Slept like a log. Can't have been drugged, surely. Then I thought, what about the pack of toilet rolls. And soap and flannel, toothpaste and toothbrush. Looking around the room where was I supposed to go to the toilet. There was no sign of a bucket. There wasn't a sink. There was a door though, that I thought was probably locked and maybe went to another room adjoining this room. So I went to the door and turned the handle. It opened and inside was a small room with a toilet and sink.

On the one hand I was much relieved, glad even, thanking my lucky stars, a toilet and sink and thank you for that. But on the other hand, all this comfort worried me. Scared me even. They had meant to keep me for a while and why else would they go to all the trouble. I looked around the room. My cell, my prison cell. The view from the window was blue sky, not a cloud that I could see in sight. Swallows, I think, the way they swooped and dived, came into view. A room with a view. And I thought about the James Bond film, it just came into my head. A View to a Kill. But they hadn't. Killed me that is. I was very much alive, shaken but not stirred. Yeah, still alive, so I had to be grateful for that. Even though I was effectively kidnapped, held prisoner in this room. I was still very much alive. I looked out the window, the blue sky.

Glad that I live am I and the sky is blue. Funny how things come back to you, like a school hymn sung, that at the time I completely ignored, bored by the school assembly and the drone of prayers and hymns. Looking back I would sing it with gusto and feel every last word. Glad that I live am I and the sky is blue.

They both came into the room, the gunman and the guy that had been driving the van. Morning had broken and most of the day had come and gone. Something was up.

'We just wanted to say we know that we got off to a bad start, maybe a bit rough and that, eh,' said the gunman, trying to be sincere, but sounding fake. And obviously the mouthpiece of the two. The driver just stood silent and smoked his cigarette, looking content to let the gunman do the talking for them.

The gunman had his gun tucked into the waistband of his cargo pants, like they do, wanna-be gangsters. I wished for the gun to go off and blow his fucking balls away, see him writhe in agony. He had designer stubble, a buzz cut and expensive white teeth. Really nice trainers. He came across vain, the type of guy that would always look in a mirror to check himself out. I would say he was around thirty years of age, something like that. The driver looked the opposite. He had thick grey hair and looked like he combed it with his hands. Jeans and a top that looked like they came from a Sunday market stall. I am guessing he was sixty-something. Though some people, and looking at him he could be one of them, some people age badly and look older than their years. He could have been less than forty and had a shit-hard life. Where the gunman was obviously from London, the driver was maybe russian, definitely eastern europe I would have to say.

'So,' said the gunman. He was holding a newspaper in his hand, rolled up like when you want to swat a fly, or bop someone over the head. 'I guess that you know why you are here, you're not stupid. If it had been a robbery, we'd have done that, robbed you, though got away with next to nothing. You don't have an expensive watch on, but you did have some money on you. Sixty-quid. What a waste of our time that would have been, eh. Sixty-quid. And there you go, waltzing out the gate, dressed in shit. Thought for a moment that you were a tradesman, gardener, painter whatever.

Couldn't believe our eyes, and our luck ...' the gunman rolled his eyes and smiled, like he had got all the numbers on the Lotto, seen his horse gallop over the line and had bet the house on it, pulled the arm on a gaming machine in Las Vegas and hit the jackpot, maybe all in one glorious day. 'Anyway. Here you are and here you will stay until we have conducted business with the appropriate people.'

So this was their cunning Baldrick plan, to hold me to ransom in the vain hope that the ransom would be paid. Well good luck on that one. Pretty sure that the police would not allow a ransom to be paid in case it encouraged copy-cats. Football clubs would have to get extra security for their players around the clock, and players and their families would hate the intrusion of that. Most players were pretty normal and liked to do normal stuff, not be shadowed everywhere by security people. The ransom plan seemed to me to be a complete non-starter, but I was not about to open my mouth and tell them so. They may have agreed and said you are right, so let's just kill him if it's a waste of our time and just another mouth to feed.

'So like I say,' said the gunman, like he was winding up the brief conversation after putting me in the picture. 'You'll be here for a while, short while hopefully. And you'll be looked after, fed and watered so as to speak, though not like an animal, eh. Good healthy food, plenty of fruit and stuff, don't want you wasting away. Obviously you will have to stay under lock and key, but you have a toilet and a sink to wash, and you can exercise. Sit ups and the like and keep yourself in shape, jog on the spot, eh.'

The gunman passed me the rolled up copy of the Evening Standard newspaper.

'Congratulations, Jack. You're a dad.' And they left the room.

8

Press conference arranged to satisfy the insatiable demands of the media over the sudden disappearance of Jack Jones.

   A full house.

   Lights, cameras, action.

   There are more questions than answers.

And the more they find out the less they know.

9

'Sit down, sergeant.'

'Yes, sir,' said sergeant Bob Smith, sitting down and looking across the desk to the Chief Superintendent, wondering why he had been called into his office so urgently.

'Now as you are aware,' said the Chief Superintendent, slowly and deliberately, keeping eye contact with the sergeant, 'we have a surge in dog-taking, dognapping, call it what you will. And as you are also aware, up to now, the perception is, we have not been taking it seriously enough. That is why I tasked you in getting a dedicated team together to tackle this issue.'

'Yes, sir,' said sergeant Bob Smith. Very aware. They had not taken it seriously enough. Not while it was not in the news that is, and making headlines. Now that it had made the headlines he had been given a handful of officers to make some headway and show that the force was taking it seriously.

'Well,' said the Chief Superintendent. 'I have to tell you now, this comes from up high, and I don't mean the PM or the Home Secretary. I mean my wife, sergeant. Very upset. And like she has pointed out, and I must say, very forcefully. If I, the Chief Superintendent, cannot do anything about it, what is the point of me sitting behind this desk. Let me explain. Last night we went for a nice quiet drink at our local. They know me, and in the main respect that when I am away from the office, when I am just a civvy, enjoying a quiet drink, I don't wish to be a sounding board for their policing problems. My shed got broken into, my bike got stolen … you get the picture. Well, I ordered my usual pint of beer for me and a glass of white wine for my wife. And my wife noticed one of our neighbours in the village, not close, more pleasant exchanges. Well anyway. The lady is crying. Really upset. So my wife turned to the landlord, Jim.

Why is she crying, Jim.

Her dog has been stolen, said Jim in reply.

And my wife was shocked. Upset and angry.

That lovely Cocker Spaniel, she said.

Yes. That lovely Cocker Spaniel that she dotes on. Loves it to bits, and all she had for company since her husband died.
Heartbreaking it is. And I know what I'd like to do to the people that go around stealing dogs …

And of course, Jim looks at me. The very man that upholds the law and is meant to catch the buggers. I didn't say anything back so as to not ruin our quiet drink, picked up our drinks and headed for a table. But my wife. She headed for the neighbour to console her. And when she came back. She looked at me with a very stern face.

Well, what are you going to do about it, she said.'

The Chief Superintendent slapped the desk.

'Double the team that you have put together. And I want results, sergeant. I want arrests and dogs back with their grieving owners.'

10

The driver came into the room, under his arm he had a small dog, a Yorkshire Terrier, which looked at me and started to bark, well more yap. He had a cup of tea, milk with no sugar, now that they know how I took my tea. He passed me the mug.

'It's hot so be careful,' he said.

I took the mug and put it onto the floor. I was sitting on the chair when he came in. I had just finished a workout, some simple exercises and more to keep me from going mad, I guess. The driver quietened the dog down and laughed as it licked his face.

'When he gets to know you, he won't bark, more lick you to death,' said the driver.

He said it more to the dog than me, I didn't want to get to know it. Not that the dog wasn't cute, just the way that he said it implied I would be here for some time. Days had passed already.

The driver went to go, but before he did he asked for the Evening Standard newspaper back. I had read it cover to cover, and as a rule

I didn't really read newspapers, especially the ones that I saw as more comics, full of tits and tittle-tattle. And reading my story, my disappearance, my wife and baby and all the other stuff, it felt like the usual coverage, kind of made up and sensational, they were writing about my life and I didn't recognize half of it, more a fucking fantasy. Reading it hadn't helped and I was glad to hand the newspaper back.

'Thank you,' said the driver.

The driver left the room. I heard the dog yap as I am guessing it was put on the floor while the driver locked the door. Then the silence. I went and laid on the sleeping bag, my bed for the duration of my stay. I closed my eyes and thought about some of the coverage in the newspaper.

A lot of speculation that Manchester United were after me, some saying that I could be the new George Best, one of their greatest players. Very flattering but I am happy to be just me, rather than compared to this player or that player. Several things stuck out though in the newspaper, I guess I had similar skills. And discovered young, very young actually. And he also disappeared. But that was down to him missing a train from Manchester to London. Manchester United were due to play Chelsea and George Best was supposed to be playing but went down to London on a later train and instead of playing he went to the flat of the actress Sinead Cusack in Islington. He holed up there for several days while the media besieged the flat waiting for him to make an appearance. And that is where I part company with the late and great George Best. Booze and women were his sad downfall. They won't be mine. And I was lucky that I stayed at home with my mum and had my family and friends around. George Best had to leave his home in Northern Ireland and make a new life in England and Manchester, living in digs while young and away from family and friends. And with my eyes closed I was suddenly asleep, just drifting away thinking about the time I went missing and my being discovered all on the same day.

We were at the seaside, staying in a borrowed bungalow, just my mum and me. The weather had been perfect, blue skies and sunshine and no rain to ruin our holiday. There were seagulls, fish and chips and glorious sand stretching for miles, well it seemed like miles at that age, seven and still in shorts. My mum and dad had recently divorced, but stayed close friends, and I was grateful for that, it meant that I could have them both in my life but just not in the same house. My dad didn't move away that far and I could see him whenever I wanted.

What cards shall I get, then.

My mum was saying it more to herself, choosing cards from a spinning rack thing. Saucy or scenic and in the end buying several of each.

Now you wait here a minute, and I won't be a mo, just go in and pay for them. I'll get us an ice cream, that will be nice. And don't move, she said, wagging her finger at me.

That would be nice, I loved ice cream, especially at the seaside in lovely weather. So I waited outside with the buckets and spades, brightly coloured inflatables and all the other seaside things that were on display to catch the eye. But the thing that caught my eye was a group of older boys bouncing a football as they walked past. And I loved football with a passion, my mum said I was born with a football at my feet, born to play the game. So I followed them, not really thinking at the time about my mum, and how she would feel coming out and me not being there. I just wanted to join in and play. And they weren't that far away really, on the sand in front of the shop where she had gone to buy her cards and get us an ice cream.

Who are you.

Jack.

Wanna play, Jack. Though you look a bit young.

He's alright, ain't you, Jack. He can go on my side.

And there were seven of them so I made up the numbers, four a side. Items of clothing for the goals and we were away with me on the field, or on the sand, because they wanted a bigger lad in goal, I was too titchy to play in goal, so they said. And although they were bigger and stronger I held my own, even scoring a couple of goals with my feet and another with my head.

Meantime.

Jack. Jack. Jack. My mum had come out and was frantically calling my name. Frantic with worry that I could have been taken by a stranger, such was my sudden disappearance.

You okay, love.

My son, Jack. I left him outside, only for a minute and told him to stay put and don't move.

How old is Jack.

Seven.

Can't have gone far. You tried the beach, what about those lads over there playing football. One looks a lot younger, is that him. Your son Jack.

My mum said that she could have kissed the lady and was really sorry that she forgot to say thank you, she was so eager to get to me. Hug me and scold me, which she did both. She made me finish my ice cream before I could carry on playing. While she watched another person had been watching the game with a keen interest. And he approached my mum.

Is that your son, the youngster playing with the older lads.

Yes. Jack.

Jack, eh. Well I have been watching your Jack play. And I have to tell you he is good, really good. Exceptional. He dribbles round them like they are not there, passes like a lad way older than his years. Quality passing. He uses both feet and has scored some cracking goals, both with his feet and his head. His balance is something else, almost supernatural the way he stays on his feet. And they are playing on sand, god knows what he is like on a football pitch. And I have to tell you that I would love to see him play on a proper football pitch.

He loves football.

And football will love him. How old is he.

Seven.

Exceptional. Let me introduce myself. Harry Roberts, chief scout at Fulham Football Club.

Mr Roberts who had been watching the game handed my mum his card. He was on holiday.

Please phone, when you get home. We can arrange for Jack to have a trial. He is very young but I would love to follow his progress.

And true to his word he did follow my progress, and when I was old enough Fulham Football Club signed me. A professional footballer with the world at my feet.

'Wake up.'

I awoke with a start. The driver was standing over me with his dog under his arm and a cigarette on the go. On the chair was a plate with my evening meal. Pasta with some sauce over it.

'Enjoy your meal. I will come back later to collect the plate. You have enough water, yes. Sure you do, I see that you filled the plastic water bottle from the tap. I will bring you another mug of tea.'

The dog did not make a sound, it was getting used to me I suppose. And used to cigarette smoke in its face no doubt. The driver left me to my evening meal. I ate the pasta and I guess I was grateful for it. I had the world at my feet, and now I was grateful for a plate of pasta, and a mug of tea to follow. Funny old world, though I wasn't laughing.

11

The gunman found a quiet spot in the woods near to the path and waited out of sight behind a tree. He smoked while he waited, puffing out the smoke and waving it away to break up the cloud as it left his mouth so as not to give himself away. Shortly an elderly lady came into view with her dog off the lead. A French Bulldog that was behind her sniffing away at the ground and a perfect size for a quick snatch.

'Come do, keep up, Lotty …' said the lady turning around and calling to her dog. The dog ignored her call and became too interested in the surroundings, the scent from other dogs that used the woods. So she kept walking, leaving Lotty to explore and do what dogs do as long the dog did not stray too far.

The gunman waited till the lady was a good few yards in front, then crept out from behind the tree and quickly grabbed the dog under his arm, with one hand over its mouth, and bolted. Until the kidnapping plan paid out they needed the ready cash that stolen dogs could provide.

Get the right breed and the right age and people bought them, no questions asked. They wanted to keep Jack for a while, let the family and Fulham Football Club sweat for a bit, and let the ransom for his release go higher each day that he was not found. They had found a place, nice and out of the way, a quality hideout, so they were happy to sit it out just so long as they had the cash to do that. And the dog under his arm would do that nicely.

12

The driver came into the room and as usual was carrying the Yorkie under his arm, with a cigarette dangling in his mouth while he held onto my mug of tea. He offered me the mug and then went and sat on the chair. The smoking chair as it had become. I sat on my bed with my back against the wall. He took the cigarette from his mouth and coughed, and the poor little dog coughed.

'Shit habit, even my dog is coughing. I should give it up, yes.'

He was talking to the dog. He then put the dog on the floor.

'You stay quiet, no noise.'

The dog, which was quite sweet, though I had always preferred larger dogs, came over to me, so I put out a hand and stroked it.

'He likes you,' said the driver, smiling.

Yeah. He liked me. The little thing then wandered around the room sniffing at things.

The driver then went out of the room for a moment, coming back with a metal waste bin.

He sat back down on the chair and put the bin at his feet. Continued with his cigarette.

The driver smoked his cigarette while in thought, seemingly miles away as the smoke curled around him, and ash fell from the burning tip. Then he looked at me. 'You like films.'

'Yeah. I guess, depending on what films though.'

'The first film that I saw the English actor Michael Caine in, I thought, why is he playing it like he is gay. It was Zulu and I could not understand why. Then I saw him in the Ipcress file and he was gay in that as well, well gay to me, with his big glasses and the way he cooked his food. Then I saw him in Get Carter and Alfie. By now I thought, he is making those films to look to the world that he is not gay, but why did it matter. So he is gay. I have a fondness for Norman Wisdom, yes. A lot of older Albanians do, it was all we could watch in Albania. Norman Wisdom films.'

So he was Albanian.

'You like Norman Wisdom.'

'Yeah, I guess. Hard not to like him. If he is on the telly I will watch his films, and yeah, they always make me laugh.'

I drank my tea. He made a nice brew, good colour and just right. So that was something. The little Yorkie came over and sat right next to me, kind of snuggled up, which was nice. When I ever get out of here maybe I will change my mind about getting a large dog.

'The Carry On films, you like them.'

I looked at the driver, imagined him with an old black and white television set from a bygone age, one of those aerials on top of the television that you had to play with to get a good picture, and he would be watching all that old stuff. In Albania cut off from the world, seeing Great Britain through the world of Norman Wisdom and the Carry On films. Must have been a shock when he arrived here. The Britain of when those films were made is long gone.

'If a Carry On film is on the telly, which they are quite a bit, yeah I may watch them, and I guess some of them are quite funny. Well the first ones, anyway. Once they got on the treadmill and churned them out they became very unfunny. I don't bother with the later ones.'

The driver blew out smoke, waved it away in an attempt to clear away the fog settling around him. He coughed loudly, making the little Yorkie look his way. 'I like the Carry On films …' and the driver started to laugh thinking about the Carry On films. The laughter turned into a coughing fit. His face went red as he coughed and for a moment I thought he was about to have a heart attack. The little Yorkie was so concerned it started to bark loudly. I didn't know what to do, apart from offer him water, which I did. Getting the water in the mug and giving it to him to drink, while the Yorkie barked at his feet. He drank the water. And the coughing eased. So did the Yorkie, as it came back and sat next to me.

'Thank you,' he said.

He then lit another cigarette as though nothing had happened.

'In London I follow Chelsea, you should play for Chelsea, you would be good for them, yes.'

'Maybe I would. But that is never gonna happen while I am kept here, is it.'

It came out surly, but then again how else could it have come out. Did he really expect me to have a chat about whether I should play for Chelsea. And my life in general, stuck here and not knowing when I will be released. Knowing little about how my family will be coping, what they would be going through, only what I had read in the Evening Standard newspaper, and that was now old news.

He stood up abruptly, and was obviously offended by my manner. He called the dog and picked it up under his arm. He then looked at me before leaving. 'You will be released soon, yes. The Chelsea owner has a lot of money, maybe he wants you to play for them. Would pay to see you released so that he could sign you. You stay in London. Manchester United will not suit you. I have been to Manchester. It rains a lot.'

'Who is that over there.'

'Dunno, mate, she came with Isabel. Go and ask Isabel, or you know what, go and ask her. Just go over to her and say, excuse me, but who are you.'

'No. It's alright,' and I swigged my beer from the bottle, trying to act cool, nonchalant, not really that interested, she was just another girl at the party.

My mate laughed. 'Who are you kidding. Acting like you are not that bothered. You've been staring at her, but pretending not to. Drinking your beer while drooling over her. She is gorgeous, mate. Go on, introduce yourself, and if you don't I will.'

I looked at him, he was right, I was being an idiot. 'Okay, I will.'

I swigged my beer, and put the bottle on a table as I walked towards her. My heart racing, going boom-diddy-boom. Now I wasn't normally like this, acting like a nervous kid, but she had cast a spell on me. When I got to her, in my head I had rehearsed what I was going to say by way of introduction. Play it cool, not too cool, say something half sensible, not a stupid chat-up line.

'Did you want something.'

I stood there, under her spell, feeling stupid. She had bewitched me, leaving me bothered and bewildered. I had lost my power of speech.

She smiled. 'Are you going to stand there all night with your mouth open, and nothing coming out.'

I looked around to my mate, grinning at me. I turned back to the girl. 'Sorry. Can I walk away, then come back and start again.'

She laughed. Not in my face, just laughed. And not at me, more the situation that she had found herself in.

I laughed, and it broke the ice.

'Want a drink.'

That was about the best opening line that I could manage. She held up a full bottle of beer, and smiled. I smiled back. 'Well I need one, be right back,' and I left her to go and get a beer. Coming back moments later. I chinked my beer bottle against her bottle. 'Cheers.'

We smiled at each other, and it felt natural to be in her company, like I had known her for years and you don't have to force yourself to talk, just for the sake of it. I didn't want to go and spoil it all by saying something stupid, like I love you. The party was at a house in trendy

East London, and it was banging. Great music and great vibe.

Some sensual soul started to come from the sound system.

'Wanna dance,' she said.

She knocked her beer back and put the bottle down. Took my arm so that I could hardly refuse. Waited while I finished my beer, then led me to where people were dancing. And we danced to the soul music and we were kind of wrapped around each other and when Marvin Gaye came out the speakers, Let's Get It On, I felt that we were almost making love, it was that sensual. Then the music changed and suddenly people were going wild dancing to a different groove.

'I need another beer now,' she said, edging away from the dancing.

'I'll get you one.'

So we stood out in the street, the party was petering out, people drifting away. I looked at her, she looked at me. 'Well, this is it, I guess.' Not really wanting the night to end.

'Yeah,' she said.

'How are you getting home, taxi or …'

'Walking. Haven't got that far to go, Bethnal Green. Nice evening, warm. Yeah I'll walk. What about you.'

'Putney. I'm gonna get a cab.'

She smiled. 'Well. Had a great time. We had a great time. You are a very good dancer … anyway …'

She kissed me on my cheek. It burnt a hole in it. I couldn't let it end here on the pavement, I just couldn't. 'Let me walk you home.'

She laughed. 'Very gallant. But you are way over the otherside of London, it's miles out of your way.'

'Please.'

She laughed some more. 'Okay.'

So we started to walk, it was a warm evening, the day had been hot, blue sky and sunshine, real Isley Brothers Summer Breeze sort of day, sweet days of summer that made you feel fine.

'What do you do, you know, for a living.'

I was kind of dreading that question. It either puts people off, no not off, just changes the situation. But I had to answer honestly, no good making something up. 'I play football.'

She looked at me kind of unsure, not like I was lying, just needed to hear it again. 'Football.'

'Yeah, football.'

'For a living, like a professional. A professional footballer. Wow. Who do you play for.'

'Fulham. Signed when I was a teenager and played for them ever since.' I changed the subject, and wanted to know more about her. 'What about you, what do you do, workwise.'

She smiled. 'Retail.'

I smiled back. 'Shopgirl.'

She playfully punched my arm. 'Actually I am a shopgirl, and there's nothing wrong with that. I enjoy it. Mr Professional footballer.'

I playfully punched her back. 'Didn't say there was. My mum works at Peter Jones in Sloane Square. Worked there for years, she loves it and sees it as her second family.'

'I don't really follow football. My dad does, he is a West Ham supporter.'

'Come on the 'ammers,' I said, trying to sound cockney.

'Forever blowing bubbles, that is what my dad says. Never win anything, just forever blowing bubbles. He was gutted when West Ham left Upton Park. Hates the way football is going, all the money in the game and taken over by foreign owners. Upton Park was part of the community and he felt that the community spirit was broken, the club was wrenched from them, whether they liked it or not.'

There was not a lot that I could say to that, so I didn't say anything. We had been walking for quite a bit and I could sense her slowing down as we got to where she lived.

'Well this is it,' she said, stopping outside a terrace house.

Where we part company. Though I didn't want the evening to end, it had to end somewhere. She was home, and I still had to get home. And I still didn't know her name. And like she was reading my mind.

'You haven't asked my name.'

'Funny you should say that, spooky actually, cos I was just about to. And get your phone number, that is if you don't mind giving it to me. I would love to maybe do something, go out, dunno. Drink maybe or …'

'Jill,' she said, 'and yeah, love to go for a drink sometime.'

And she went to get her phone out from her crossbody bag. And looked a bit put out as I laughed loudly. Not loud enough to wake the street, but loud enough. I put out my hand to introduce myself. 'Jack,' I said.

She immediately got it and laughed as well. Took my hand and squeezed it, like it was meant to be. Jack and Jill.

'What are you drinking,' I asked Jill.

'What are you drinking,' she said back.

'I was going to have a pint.'

'Well I'll have the same, a pint as well.'

We had agreed to meet in a pub for our first date, and it was a really agreeable local near to where she lived. I ordered our beers then brought them to a bench seat where Jill had sat down, the pub had a nice feel to it and was mainly used by locals, old and young. And it was the kind of pub where the people left you alone, even if they recognised you, they respected your privacy, probably why Jill had chosen it so we wouldn't be bothered by people. I had grown used to people wanting to come and chat with me, take a selfie, that sort of stuff. But it could be a pain, sometimes, when you really just wanted to be left alone.

It was a lovely moment when she turned up. She had a warm smile on her face, looked really fab in her flowery vintage 70s dress worn with simple pumps, her hair in a classic French plait. How would I describe her, just beautiful, I guess. I saw her face in a crowded place, and knew that it was meant to be.

And we chatted away, easy in our own company, getting to know one another by talking about what we liked, disliked, asking questions, not grilling, just getting to know each other through shared things that maybe we had in common. Family background was pretty similar and our passions seemed to entwine, as I found out.

'You are joking,' she said, her face lit up. 'Wow, that is incredible.'

'Yeah. Imagine that. I got a bronze and was elated. Was more than happy with that and didn't go for the silver or gold, football was starting to take up all my time and was getting more serious, I knew that I had to concentrate on it full time. But I would never have not done it, not for the world.'

She had told me how she had entered the Duke of Edinburgh Awards when she was a teenager. How it had changed her life and had gone all the way to gold. What a small world. Amazing that we had both entered the Duke of Edinburgh Awards.

'I now go into schools and tell them about my experience and encourage kids to go on the courses as they are life changing in so many ways.' I picked up her empty glass. 'Gold, eh. That deserves another drink. Still on beer and a pint.'

'Yeah, why not. And a packet of crisps, please.'

'What flavour.'

'Plain, please.'

While I was at the bar ordering two pints and a packet of crisps, I had an idea. To see if she was game to share a passion of mine, and maybe I would share something that she loved to do. Both have a go, within reason. So when I sat back down with our beer and her crisps I put it to her. And she was dead keen on the idea. But obviously had certain reservations.

'That sounds really cool,' she said. 'But just one thing, I am not jumping out of planes, no way am I skydiving or parachuting from a plane, sorry, not gonna happen.'

I laughed. 'Shooting,' I said. 'Clay pigeon.'

'Wow. Didn't see that coming.'

And she seemed genuinely surprised. And relieved that it was something done with both feet on the ground.

'Can't imagine you in a flat cap and Barbour jacket.' She laughed. 'No don't see it. Still. If that is your thing, I would love to give it a go. Why not. Sounds fun, though I have never done it before, no, it sounds brilliant.' She then pulled a face, looked serious. 'So long as it is just shooting at clays.'

'Definitely just clays. And I would not in a million years enjoy blasting birds out of the sky, couldn't think of anything worse. Killing wildlife for sport is really not my thing.'

She kissed me on my cheek. 'Thank fuck for that, for a moment I was worried that you did all that stuff, the shooting and hunting thing. I seriously would have had to walk away. Can't bear cruelty to animals, especially in the name of sport. Couldn't be with a guy that did that.'

I smiled and kissed her back. 'Sorted that out then, and another thing we have in common. Wildlife should be left alone to be wild. Now it's your turn to surprise me.' And I grinned, I was game for a laugh.

She picked her beer up and drank some. Put the glass down and wiped her mouth. 'Nice beer,' she said. 'Right, my turn. And it is something that I have been doing for ages and absolutely love it with a passion. I go with a group of friends and I can't describe how good it is for the soul, as well as incredibly healthy. I just love it. Wild swimming. So. Are you up for that.'

'Yeah, too right. Of course. Definitely. Wild swimming. I mean, I have kind of done that, swimming in rivers.'

She smiled. 'Yeah I guess most people have at some time. But not everyone actively engages in it, otherwise the places we find would be like a lido in summer and full with people. It's being at one with nature and completely alone with just your group of friends. And amazingly there are some fabulous places just like that near London. The Surrey and Sussex hills are super rich in secret wooded pools. Just incredible. A lot of people will seek out water in the summer, to cool down. But when you go in the autumn, the solitude is just breathtaking. And winter, that is a whole new experience, love the winter swims …' she laughed. 'Sorry, sounding a bit zealous. But I did say I love it with a passion.'

'Great,' I said. 'And all I need is swimming trunks.'

And she laughed, joyously. Made a pretend shotgun and fired off two shots, bang, bang. 'All I need is a gun.'

I parked near where Jill was living and walked to her door. She came out with a big smile on her face, and did a twirl on the pavement to show off her attire, a borrowed flat cap and oversized Barbour jacket.

'Like my shooting gear,' she said, laughing.

'A lot,' I said. She looked gorgeous, was gorgeous, could wear a potato sack and look stunning. 'Like it a lot …' and I laughed with her. Both laughing on the pavement, her laughter was infectious and something that I already loved about her.

We walked to my pickup truck, I had a thing about pickup trucks. Early American. I had a 1970 cream and dark red Ford F100 restored and converted to right hand drive. It was a peach and I loved it. So did Jill, smiling wide as she slid over near me on the bench seat and kissed me.

'I have something for you,' I said, as I got the surprise gift from the glove box. 'I hope you like it.'

She tugged at the ribbon and slowly unwrapped the present on her lap, and looked seriously pleased as she discovered what I had bought her. She held it in her hands for a moment just staring at it, then kissed me full on the mouth. 'Love it,' she said. 'Seriously, I just love it. You don't know what this means, I feel really touched … just feels so special …' and she kissed me again.

'Put it on,' I said. Really happy that she genuinely loved it as much as I did. It was a yellow silk cravat with a design of shotgun cartridges printed on it that I had bought from Holland and Holland in London. I watched as she wrapped it around her neck, and looked in the large interior mirror to get it just right.

She smiled wide at her reflection and the cravat. 'Love it,' she said. 'So fab, seriously cool.'

'Good,' I said, as I turned over the engine and we pulled away.

We drove out of London and just thirty miles away was my shooting club where I was a member. It was set in forty-acres of woodland and was stunning. Had great layouts, for the experienced and the novice. And dedicated instructors trained to the highest standard and extremely knowledgeable. It was where I kept my shotgun, a Blaser F3 Vantage, in safe storage under lock and key, there when I needed it. I had my gear in a bag on the back seat that I would need for the day, shooting glasses, ear defenders and cartridge pouch and a shooting vest. The club would provide Jill with whatever she needed so that she could have a good days shooting, including a personal instructor that I had booked to get her shooting her first clays. I personally could not wait to see her face, at the thrill of squeezing the trigger and downing the first clay, watching it shatter in the sky.

I stood and watched as Jill went through her lesson with the instructor, after firstly choosing a suitable gun for her size and build. Going through the safety rules, how to load and getting used to the recoil as the shot is fired. Explaining the gun fit, when choosing the right gun. And eye dominance, which eye was best used to follow the clay as you took aim. Concentrating on posture and generally getting confidence on handling the gun, before having a go at the first shot. The instructor explained that they would use what was called a floppy crow, the target clay was a slow, near vertical clay, giving the novice plenty of time to become visually aware.

Then it was time for her first clay, she looked at me and smiled, made sure that her ear defenders were correctly on, then looked down the barrel of the gun and waited for the clay. Bang, and the clay broke into pieces. Her face lit up and she squealed with delight. She lifted her ear defenders as the instructor praised her, and looked around to me.

'Smashed it. You are a natural,' I said. And couldn't be happier that she was enjoying it so much.

She laughed. 'Lucky first shot.'

She was right, it was a lucky first shot as she missed the next half a dozen clays. But then she hit one, and the next. Clay after clay were shattered by the shot as she gained in confidence. So she was a natural after all. Now that I could see that she was really enjoying it and thrilled by the experience, I left to go and do some shooting of my own.

I looked out the window, outside looked sludgy grey and chilly, an overcast October morning. I had my bag open on the bed and the gear that I would need spread over the bed ready to pack, for my first taste of wild swimming. I slowly packed what I needed, what Jill had said that I would need. A winter wetsuit and socks, anti-chafing lubricant, goggles and earplugs, and a cap just in case. And a waterproof changing robe, which was a must when getting out from the cold water. I packed a large towel as well and made sure that I had warm clothes for after the swim. She had talked about a float but she was a strong swimmer and preferred without, and I was also pretty confident that I would not need one. And she was going to bring a flask with something hot to drink. With the bag full and satisfied that I pretty much had everything, I went for a shower, then I would get dressed and jump in the pickup and go and pick-up Jill for our big adventure, one that I was looking forward to.

We arrived at our destination, somewhere that Jill knew well and would be quiet at this time of year, a beautiful stretch of river and quite secluded, as we drove down a track through a wooded area, the trees still in leaf and ablaze with autumn colours. We came out onto a stretch of grass that led to the river and could park safely with the river in view. A weak sun had started to appear in the sky, slowly burning away the cheerless grey of the morning. This stretch of the river slowly meandered through the unspoilt surrounding countryside and a perfect place to swim. You could wade in safely and push yourself out into mid stream and at once be at one with nature.

Jill could see it in my face how I thought about the secluded spot. 'What did I tell you,' she said.

'Yeah, you were right. It's like paradise, really beautiful … listen,' I said, standing for a moment hushed. 'All you can hear is the birds and the gentle sound of the river. So peaceful. Just beautiful.'

'Let's get our wetsuits on and get in the water,' said Jill, getting her bag from the back seat of the pickup.

I got my bag and we slowly undressed. Before we put on our wetsuits we put on anti-chafing lubricant, helping each other get to the hard to reach bits, which was fun.

'Wait to you get in the chilly water, that will stop you getting aroused,' said Jill, laughing.

And it was cold, fucking freezing even with wetsuits, as I slid into the water on my backside. But I was in the river and soon we were swimming alongside each other and you quickly forgot the cold. It was so exhilarating, and Jill was so right and I could now see why she was so passionate about it. Just you and nature all to yourself, the slowly moving river and the autumn colours of the trees in the dappled sunlight. Beautiful.

So. We had a shotgun wedding, that was an absolute blast. Then for our honeymoon we went wild swimming in Italy. Where we found waterfalls, turquoise and emerald rock pools, crystal clear rivers gently flowing in gorgeous landscapes. It was a wild and fun adventure. We loved it.

I woke up and looked around me, at four dark walls that surrounded me, yeah, I had been dreaming.

Outside there was a raging storm. Thunder exploded in the black sky, lightning crackled and the rain pelted noisily on the roof and window. It added to the grim situation that I had found myself in, the loud fireworks outside a soundtrack to a chilling film. One that I was grimly staring in.

'Stop him …' the police officer shouted loudly to his colleague as he saw the person that they were after bolting from an alley.

The other police officer gave chase, running down the street after the man holding a puppy under his arm, a puppy that the police officers believe to be stolen less than twenty-minutes before, and as a unit put together to solve dog crime, they were quickly on the scene of the distressed young lady that had had her newly bought puppy stolen in broad daylight while walking it in her local park. The two undercover police officers drove around the area looking for the person based on the description that the tearful young lady had managed to give them, and on seeing someone fit that description, carrying a puppy under his arm, quickly pulled over, got out of the car and gave chase. Losing him in a side street before seeing him appear from an alley.

The gunman, on hearing the loud shout from a police officer, and quickly seeing another police officer within a short distance from him, dropped his shoulders and quickened his pace, determined to get away and keep the valuable puppy at any cost. And there in front of him was his chance, and never one to look a gift horse in the mouth he took it. A terrace house with the door open and a person from the house, an elderly man, cleaning his downstairs window with a bucket of water and a cloth. The gunman darted into the house, slammed the door shut and bolted it from the inside. Quickly made his way through the house to the back door and the garden, while the officer banged on the front door, as his breathless colleague caught up and looked frantically for another way into the house, with the elderly man pointing to an alley yards away that would take them to the rear.

The gunman meanwhile had opened the back gate and got into the adjoining back garden from across the alley that ran down the back of the terrace street. He banged on the window and a startled lady appeared at her back door, before she had a chance to speak, the gunman pushed past her and came out from her front door. Where his next lucky encounter happened. A deliveroo guy on a scooter had just pulled up with a takeaway meal. The gunman, seeing his chance, and quick on his feet, as well as his ability to think and act quickly, pulled his gun and ordered the young guy to hand over his helmet and keys to the scooter and the bag on his back. Which the terrified young guy did, and on being told to go, he did just that and turned and ran. The gunman then opened the insulated bag, got the meal out and chucked it on the pavement and put the puppy inside, doing the bag up but leaving a gap so the puppy could breathe, put the deliveroo bag on his back, got on the scooter and made his escape.

'The tea is good, yes. A nice cup of tea.'

I looked at the mug of tea, what could I say, the colour was just right, it tasted good. The driver made a nice cup of tea. 'Yeah, thank you.'

The driver looked pleased, he seemed to like compliments, whether the tea or his food. He went and sat on the chair and got out a cigarette, the smoking chair. I was brought up to be polite, say thank you, though not sure that my mum meant for me to go this far, to be so polite to my kidnappers. Though she was right, good manners did not cost anything, and better to keep on the right side of them than not. And he had brought me an unexpected treat. A KitKat. I would save the chocolate treat for later, eat it on my own. I didn't fancy eating it while he was watching, and anyway, I really didn't want to share it with the Yorkie that he put down onto the floor as he came into the room, and was curled up next to me. So I sipped my tea, and stared at the floor, while he silently smoked his cigarette.

Smoke curled up to the ceiling, and drifted around the room, while the driver sat silently smoking, seemingly miles away deep in thought. Though I knew he would start a conversation soon enough, it had become his habit to come into the room and want to talk, maybe through boredom while they waited. Waited to exchange me for what they hoped that they would get for me, the money for their new and better life, I guess, and for me my freedom. And I was right, he looked at me, and his mouth opened and smoke escaped as he began his conversation.

'Do you like art, paintings, yes.'

Did I like art, which was a better question than, do you want that KitKat. Did I like art, like paintings. Well it depended on the painting, some I liked, really liked and others not so much.

'Yeah, I guess. Some. I like the National Portrait Gallery, and Tate Britain. Tate Modern is a great place for a visit, but a lot of the stuff leaves me cold if I'm honest. Not one for conceptual stuff and splatter paintings. I never get them. So …'

'Not your cup of tea.'

'No.'

He finished his cigarette, dropped it into the metal bin. I would pick up the bin after he had left the room and flush it away down the toilet. I could ask him to do that, but no big deal, anyway, it gave me something to do.

'Have you a favourite painting. When you visit a gallery. Is there one that you admire, that holds your attention.'

Actually, there was one painting that I admired and held my attention. So much so I bought a poster of it and had it framed. I call it the tit and the dog, as a joke. It is a painting by Lucian Freud, Girl with a White Dog. The dog is an English Bull Terrier and is just so incredibly life-like. You can stare at the dog and it stares back at you, its gaze follows you as it lays on the bed with the Girl, looking at you and inviting you to reach out and stroke it, and say nice dog, you good dog you, while trying to ignore the Girl exposing one breast as she too stares out from the canvas.

'Lucian Freud, Girl with a White Dog.'

The driver smiled. Got another cigarette and lit it. Puffed out smoke. 'Girl with a White Dog. I too like Lucian Freud and I know the painting. Maybe we went to the same exhibition at the Tate, who knows, yes. The Girl in the painting that you so like was his first wife, Kitty Garman. He painted her many times. I will tell you my favourite painting, from an artist that I knew well. A famous artist that is no longer with us, only his work is left for people to admire. Maybe you too have seen his work, though whether you admire his work is another thing, maybe not your cup of tea.'

'Maybe not,' and I drank my tea, which really was my cup of tea, well mug.

The driver took a long drag on his cigarette, slowly blowing the smoke towards the ceiling. His face went reflective, sad. 'Zuber Shala. Not only a great painter, but a great man. He loved his country, Albania, and was proud to be an Albanian. He fought and died as an Albanian. His work is known all over the world, his paintings hang in many countries. His last known work was the best thing that he ever did, all his work came from the heart, his last painting came from his heart and soul, he poured all his emotions into the painting, like he knew it would be his last painting. He died soon after. I was with him to the end and witnessed that last work of art. Was there when he was killed at the hands of the Serbian army, and the only one alive that knows the full story of that last great work of art that Zuber Shala painted.'

The driver stopped. Took a long drag on his cigarette, and as the smoke escaped he stared at me while he lifted his shirt to reveal his upper body, the scarred skin from bullet wounds, as he slowly pointed to them, one by one. He pulled his shirt back down.

'I was left for dead, all of my comrades in arms were dead, including Zuber Shala. They would have finished me off with a bullet to the head to make sure that I was dead, but an American fighter plane suddenly flew overhead and they left in a hurry to get away. I could hear them shouting in panic as they left before the fighter plane came back. I must have blacked out, when I came round I was in a hospital bed.

I never asked how I had got there, I was just grateful that I had been spared to tell the tale. The story of that last known piece of work, hanging untitled. Red Garage Floor.'

I finished my tea as he talked, and put the mug down on the floor. I had an image in my head of the gallery where I had gone with Jill, and the large canvas of red that I had stared at and the name Zuber Shala came back to me. The Albanian painter that had painted the canvas in a mad daubing of red with a corner left grey.

'This painting,' I said slowly. 'That you have talked about, his last known work. Zuber Shala. Was it a large canvas of red with an area of grey left in the corner. Because if it is, I have seen it in London at an exhibition of his work.'

The driver finished his cigarette and dropped the remains in the metal bin. 'Yes that is the painting and I too went to see it hanging there in all its painful glory. Is a small world I could have stood next to you.'

The driver slowly rose to his feet. He coughed with his hand over his mouth. The Yorkie pricked his ears and got up, went to him and the driver lifted him into his arms, letting the dog lick his face while he laughed. I offered him the mug back and said thank you. He took it back with the Yorkie tucked under his arm. He looked at me before leaving the room.

'I will tell you the story of the Red Garage Floor another time. And before I go I have one thing to ask.'

I looked at his serious face wondering what he had wanted to ask me, hoping it would not be grim.

'Do you want that KitKat.'

The gunman and the driver stared at the money on the kitchen table. A small pile of notes and coins.

'Two-thousand and sixty-four pounds, and eighty-six pence,' said the gunman. 'Not bad. Not a king's ransom I know, but it'll keep us going till I nick another dog, eh.'

'You say so,' said the driver, his eyes on the money.

'Yeah, I say so.'

'Okay,' said the driver, 'but first we need to take out our expenses. Then we know how much money we have.'

The gunman took a cigarette out from his packet of cigarettes on the table. He lit it and took a long drag. Puffed out the smoke in little rings that floated gently away. Watched as the driver counted out the money into piles.

'Rent,' said the driver. 'Food.'

The gunman held his cigarette in one hand and pointed to the cash for food with his other hand. 'That includes dog food for your poxy dog as well as the nicked dogs I take it.'

The driver shook his head. Lit a cigarette of his own. Looked at the gunman with cold eyes.

The gunman smiled. 'Just saying,' he said.

'Well don't,' said the driver. And carried on dividing the money. 'Petrol. Shopping. Miscellaneous items. The Polaroid camera was a hundred and thirty pounds.'

The gunman looked at the money that was left. He picked up a biscuit tin and took off the lid then put the remaining cash into it, got up from the table and put the biscuit tin in a kitchen wall cupboard.

The driver put the other money into a plastic tupperware box and handed it to the gunman, who placed it next to the biscuit tin. That done, they both sat down again and finished their cigarettes. While a radio played in the background.

As a song started the gunman got up and turned the radio volume up. It was Matt Monro, Softly As I Leave You. He stood and listened to the song, and looked quite emotional as The Man with the Golden Voice filled the kitchen. As the song finished he turned the radio volume down.

'Always gets me when I hear that. My mum wanted that song played at her funeral. There wasn't a dry eye. She loved Matt Monro. Best voice in the business and better than any of them, she would say. Better than Frank Sinatra and all the others.'

The gunman sat back down. Stubbed his finished cigarette into a saucer used as an ashtray. Went back to the business at hand. He picked up a Biro and opened up a pad. 'Right,' he said. 'Jack has been with us for ten days. We've established that a transfer fee for him, going by what the papers say, could be a hundred to a hundred and fifty million. Just saying it sounds stupid. That much for a footballer today. Neymar went for over two-hundred million quid. I mean, the Brazilian is a world-class player, but that amount of money. Crazy …' he scribbled down on the pad the transfer fee for Jack. 'They stand to lose the transfer fee if they don't get Jack back. So obviously they will be more than willing to part with ten-percent I would say, so …' the gunman scribbled that amount down. Ten-percent of the transfer fee. 'A hundred and fifty million pounds is the transfer fee, agreed …' and the gunman looked at the driver to check that they were still on the same page. The driver nodded to confirm that he was still in agreement so that was good enough. 'So. We settle for ten-percent. Fifteen million and seven and a half million each. Not too greedy. And we still agree with the plan. We wait a while and make them sweat then take a Polaroid with Jack holding a daily newspaper and make contact. And take nothing less than ten-percent of the amount that we have agreed on. Okay.'

The driver slowly rose to his feet and got out his cigarettes. He lit one and took a long drag. Exhaled the smoke towards the ceiling. 'Okay,' he said. The fingers that held the cigarette were nicotine stained, as were his teeth. The constant smoking had given his face an unhealthy pale appearance, a deathlike pallor, the colour of cigarette ash.

The gunman rose to his feet. 'Nearly forgot.' He left the kitchen and came back moments later with two cartons of cigarettes. He put them on the table. 'A bullseye you owe me.'

The driver looked at the cartons of cigarettes, and looked at the gunman. 'Speak English.'

The gunman laughed. 'Fifty-quid.'

The driver put a hand into his pocket and pulled out a battered leather wallet. He got out two twenty-pound notes and a ten-pound note and handed them over.

The gunman took the money and winked at the driver. 'Cheers, bud. All square, eh.'

13

The driver came into the room as I sat on the bed staring at the walls of my prison, and for a moment refused to look at him, or acknowledge him. He didn't say anything so I guess he knew how I must have felt. The desire to escape. The frustration of knowing how futile it was. To take a gamble on overpowering the driver and hope that I could evade the gunman somehow. I knew it was a dangerous fantasy and could get killed if I tried it and then I would never see my family again. So for the sake of my family as much as myself there was little that I could do. Just hope that somehow it would resolve itself with me being freed. He put the Yorkie down on the floor and it came straight to me and curled up alongside like it wanted to comfort me. They say that dogs show empathy and the little dog definitely did as it snuggled up. And I stroked it and felt immediately better for it as it licked my hand.

'Here, I have brought you tea.'

I took the mug of tea and thanked him. I thought of my mum. I will put the kettle on, she would say, a nice cup of tea will right the world.

The driver sat down on the smoking chair, and immediately got a cigarette in his mouth and lit. He sat in silence with a satisfied face enjoying his smoke.

I sat and drank my tea enjoying the warmth of the Yorkie against my leg, it was turning into my little soul mate.

'Tonight I will cook Tave me Presh ska Mish, a meatless leek bake. You may have noticed that I do not bring you food with meat in it, or fish.'

I had noticed the meals were meat free and fish free, but didn't really think that much about it or was about to question it. I was just happy to be given a meal and anyway they were quite tasty, the driver was a good cook. Jill was a great cook and liked to have mainly vegetable dishes so I was quite used to it. I could happily eat Mediterranean vegetables and pasta for every meal. But I do enjoy meat, especially a Sunday roast.

'I will not eat meat or fish and will not cook it either. I will tell you why.'

The driver took a long pull on his cigarette, settled himself into the smoking chair for the tale he was about to tell me. Haddock and lamb and why he gave it up. I wasn't going anywhere so I settled myself on the bed and got ready for his story.

'When I was a child growing up I lived on a farm, a small holding with many animals. Cows and pigs, goats and of course chickens, that would roam free in the fields and woods. We had horses to pull carts and I suppose you could say we were very backward and poor, making a living on our piece of land. But I loved my life and the Albanian countryside is very beautiful. And I loved the animals. I would give them all names and spend many happy hours in the company of them. Collect the eggs, help milk our cows and the goats. Spend time in the pen with the pigs. I would talk to the animals and was convinced that they could talk back like they were my friends. So when it was time for an animal to be killed it broke my heart. I could not face a plate of meat put in front of me. My mother was a very understanding lady as well as loving. She would not force me to eat meat and would make vegetable meals for me. She was a wonderful cook so I did not miss out. To this day I cannot eat meat without thinking of the animal that suffered.'

It sounded very much like what I had read about Paul McCartney and how he had watched the lambs gamboling in the fields and looked at the roast lamb that they were about to eat and decided that they would go veg. I am guilty like most people of not really linking the animal with the food on the plate. A pig is a pig and a sausage, a sausage, or bacon. I look at a plate of lamb cutlets and don't see a lamb gamboling.

The driver started to cough, and coughed for a good few seconds before getting up and going into the toilet. I heard him bring up phlegm and spit into the bowl, then after he bent over the sink and drank some water from the cold tap. He had left his cigarette on the chair with the lit end hanging over the edge so as not to burn it. He came back and picked it up and sat back down. Resumed his smoking till the cigarette was finished.

'When I was looking for work some years ago I was offered a job on a trawler. They said that the pay was good so I took it. I had an image in my head of being at sea and a fisherman, a noble pursuit, people have gone to sea for thousands of years to bring back fish to feed the people. But the image in my head was not the reality. It was a giant factory ship and industrial fishing on a vast scale. I worked in the bowels of the ship as the fish was sent down to us and it was like a living hell. There were many people from many countries and we were treated like slaves. I witnessed the catches. The fish being plundered and the many fish that were caught up in the nets that were not being used but thrown back as nothing but waste, many of them protected fish. It sickened me to see so much destruction of our seas, to see a noble pursuit turned into a floating factory raping the seas. I vowed that when I got back on shore that I would never eat fish again such was the horror that I had witnessed. So that is why I do not eat fish.'

The driver lit another cigarette. He sounded anguished as he talked about his time at sea. The memories obviously left a scar. He painted a vivid picture and one that I was already aware of, because we had watched a documentary on Netflix called Seaspiracy. A friend had said if we watched it we would give up eating fish. Not unless you caught it yourself with a rod and line or from small boats that only fished in a sustainable way. I thought, yeah right, fat chance. Good luck on that. Friday night would not be Friday night without fish and chips, and London was blessed with some great places. Poppie's was a favourite and Toff's just to name two. So Jill and I put on Netflix and watched Seaspiracy. And after we looked at each other with the same thought in mind, that was it for Cod or Haddock and Friday fish and chips. I went straight to the freezer and got out a box of Waitrose fish fingers and put them in the bin, and I love Cod or Haddock fish fingers in a sandwich and it was fucking painful but the documentry was that powerful I had to do it.

The driver got up to go. And the Yorkie sensing it was time to leave went to him. I gave him back the empty mug and thanked him again for the tea. Listened as the key turned in the lock and was left alone again.

Red Garage Floor

Summer is beautiful in my homeland, trees in late summer will be heavy with fruit, the valleys and the mountains are spectacular, and the rivers and lakes that are a paradise for children to swim and fish are crystal clear.

    Zuber Shala and I grew up together as we were from the same village, his family farmed the land as we did. We roamed the fields and forests through summer and swam in the cool rivers and lakes. It was an idyllic childhood. We both married local girls and then we went our separate ways. Zuber Shala followed his chosen path to be an artist. I worked away so that I could bring back money so that we could start a family. While working away my wife left me for another man and because of the bad blood between us I left and it was many years before I returned. Zuber Shala was making it in the artworld, becoming famous. But tragedy struck when his beautiful wife died from cancer and like me he was to remain single and childless. He carried his wife in his heart and I did not and only returned to our village when she too died. I made peace with the man that had taken my young wife from me. He was a good man and they had found love and he was broken by her death. Heavy is the heart that mourns the death of a loved one.

And heavy is the heart as I talk about my homeland. How the idyllic memories from my childhood were broken by the war with Serbia. Leading to a campaign of terror, murder, rape and arson. The expulsion of hundreds of thousands of Kosovo Albanians, hundreds of thousands of my people displaced and many thousands killed. When I warmly embraced Zuber Shala little did we know that our return to our homeland would be to take up weapons and fight. We were not members of the Kosovo Liberation Army, we were ordinary men that had returned to fight to protect our villages and wage a war the best way that we could against a Serbian army and paramilitary units that were trying to wipe us from the face of the earth.

We would have to take to the mountains and the forests and use the advantage of knowing the land and where to hide and fight. We would strike and retreat and vanish into the countryside that we knew and where we could be safe.

Safe deep in the forests, and felt safe enough to light campfires so that we could cook and warm our bones when the nights were cold.

'Can you hear that,' said Zuber Shala, suddenly alert to a noise coming from the dark forest. He stood up and raised his hand to silence us. Looked to where the sound had come from. Like the noise from a large animal and could be a bear as we picked up our guns. Out from the forest a young man staggered towards us then collapsed to his knees. Zuber Shala and several men went straight to him and helped him to his feet and brought him to the campfire and sat him down. We let him recover, he was young, maybe sixteen, he was pale and broken by whatever he had gone through, fear was in his eyes and we worried for his mental well-being.

'You must eat,' I said. And I got him a plate of warm vegetable stew, which he ate hurriedly. He then drank from a bottle of beer that was put in his trembling hands. We waited. The light from the campfire lit his face and it looked like his eyes had sunken into their sockets. Then he started to talk. Slowly and painfully as he told us his story as we gathered around him in silence to hear.

He had only come out from hiding in the forest when he heard voices and he knew that we were his kinfolk and not Serbian forces. He had been walking for days and nights away from his village to escape after it was attacked by a paramilitary unit. Hiding in the forest and living off the land by eating wild berries and other fruit. Caught fish with his bare hands and ate them raw. He had lost track of time but knew it was many days and this was his first hot meal. He was grateful for the cooked meal and the beer and the fact that he stumbled across us. He would need another beer before he could tell us what had happened to his village.   Beer was scarce and rationed, each man could only hold a couple of bottles or so in their possession, but willing hands gave him what he had asked for. He then smoked his first cigarette in days. Before telling us what had happened to his village.

'We awoke to the sound of gunfire and we knew immediately that we were under attack. My grandparents were out in the fields, they were always up before sunrise busy with chores. I got my twin sister and told her she must hide. We went to the garage. I took her to the corner of the red painted concrete floor and hid her under a large grey tarpaulin. I made her promise that she would not come out until it was safe to do so. I said that I was going to get a shotgun and help the men that had gathered from the scattered properties to try and fight. We knew that the paramilitary unit would be heading for the village and we would do our best to try and stop them.

That was futile. We were heavily outnumbered by men and weapons and quickly taken prisoners. They held us at gunpoint while the village and surrounding properties were searched and people found hiding brought to the main square in the village. The elderly and small children and babies were put into the backs of trucks and driven away. I saw my grandparents amongst them and was so relieved that I openly wept. Then they separated the men from the remaining women and girls. And made us watch as they were raped in the open square in front of husbands, their cousins and uncles and brothers. The paramilitary unit were a drunken rabble, drunk on looted alcohol and their victory.

One had a glass jar with liquid and in the liquid that was used to preserve them were eyes like pickled eggs. He held up the jar towards me along with a hunting knife as if to say that I was next, that he would take out my eyes with that large knife waving in my face. Another had a glass jar with gold teeth that had been taken from the mouths of the dead. He rattled the jar while he drank from a stolen bottle of wine, like he was making music with it as he drunkenly sang aloud.

The men that had been herded together like cattle were suddenly and without warning fired at. I fell to the ground and bodies fell on top of me. I was still alive but played dead. I prayed that they would not push us into an open hole and bury me alive. But I could hear them leaving to join in with the drunken looting, and the torching of properties. As it grew dark I pushed my way out from the pile of the dead that lay over me and made my escape to the sound of shouting and singing, the sky red from the flames as my village burnt.'

'Could you take us back to your village. To see if we can find anyone else that may have survived. Your sister could still be alive and safe,' said Zuber Shala, as he reached out and placed a hand on his shoulder to comfort the young man.

The young man finished his beer. Then finished his cigarette, throwing the remains into the campfire. He sighed heavily. 'I will take you as far as the village then I will go. I want to believe that my sister escaped like I did. I have to believe that. To hold onto that. Then I have to try and find my grandparents. They brought us up after our parents died in a car accident.'

'I understand,' said Zuber Shala. 'We go in the morning. Get some sleep.'

A blanket was brought for the young man and he was soon asleep.

'The paramilitary unit will be long gone,' said Zuber Shala to the gathered men. 'We will take twelve men.'

Zuber Shala handpicked twelve men including me. The rest of the men would stay behind until our return.

The village was in the far distance when we said our farewell to the young man. He embraced each man in turn, and we wished him well and great success in finding his grandparents and assured him that he would be reunited with them and his sister. We had given him a rucksack to carry provisions for his journey, including a blanket to keep him warm as he slept under the stars. Also a hunting knife and cigarettes and matches. And a handgun that though old, still fired well, with a full pouch of bullets should he need them.

When we came to the village it was what we had expected after an attack by a lawless paramilitary unit. Homes were burnt to the ground and still smouldering, other homes had blackened wooden beams exposed, charred skeletons of what once were roofs with the tiles collapsing into the interior. Some homes remained untouched. Possessions were left that had little value, scattered amongst the debris. We came across the men that were pushed together and shot where they stood. All that was left was a pile of ash and charred skeletons. A can of empty petrol was found nearby that had been used to soak the bodies before setting them alight. It was a sickening site but to be honest one that we expected and were used to. We would begin the task of burying them. Tools were found and sleeves were rolled up for the job in hand as we dug a long trench that would take many hours of hard toil but had to be done to honour the dead. Prayers were said at the finish. May they rest in peace. We then began the task of going from home to home to see if there were any living souls left. And to find the sister of the young man if she was still alive. But we prayed that she had escaped like her brother so that the family could be reunited.

As night fell we abandoned our search in the village and surrounding homes. The occupants had fled or were taken prisoners. Animals were abandoned and left to fend for themselves, others were killed and dogs roamed wild looking for food. We too took from the deserted homes what we could use to supplement our provisions like tinned food and vegetables from the soil and fruit from trees. A campfire was made using the wood that had been chopped and piled ready for the winter. I cooked a vegetable stew that the men ate heartily. And we slept in the open air. The next day we would begin to widen the search of the properties that lay further afield.

We awoke to the sound of loud crowing coming from a cockerel, strutting around with chickens scratching at the soil for food. We would have eggs for our breakfast, along with fruit and black coffee. We ate the morning meal, washed under a hand pump and made ourselves ready to search the outlying properties scattered around. Before leaving we doused the campfire, then set off on our quest to find anyone still alive.

We came across the property by chance. It was set at the bottom of a secluded valley, surrounded by rolling hills and secret forests. The outbuildings were old and built from stone. The house and the garage were built from brickwork and then rendered and painted, with red tiled roofing. It remained to the eye untouched by the paramilitary unit.

We split up and started to search. I was in one of the outbuildings where the farm machinery was kept.

'Come quickly,' shouted one of the men, as he ran into the outbuilding. 'I think we have discovered the hiding place of the sister. This is the property for sure.'

I quickly followed him. The men had gathered at the garage. Their face coverings made me fear the worst, the smell of death hung over them like a toxic cloud. I went to the open doors of the garage. The garage was exactly as the brother had described it. Red garage floor with a grey tarpaulin in one corner.

Zuber Shala put his hand up. 'Wait,' he said. 'I will go in alone.'

We watched, heartbroken to a man, as Zuber Shala made his way slowly to the tarpaulin. He carefully pulled it away. And there she lay. She had been too frightened for her life to leave the hiding place. 24 to 72 hours after death the internal organs decompose. 3 to 5 days and the body starts to bloat. Blood-containing foam leaks from the mouth and nose. 8 to 10 days and the body turns from green to red as the blood decomposes, and organs in the abdomen accumulate gases. We now knew that she had lain there alone for at least 10 days.

We wrapped her in the tarpaulin and carried her outside.

'We have to bury her,' said one of the men.

Zuber Shala had walked away and was gone for a short time. When he returned he told us to pick up the body and to follow him. We followed with tools to dig her resting place.

He had looked at the surrounding hills and chosen a suitable place to bury her. We climbed the hill and took it in turns to carry her with six men needed, three either side. At the top we found a beautiful spot. Overlooking the property below in the valley. There she would lay undisturbed.

We dug the hole and laid her gently onto the soil, then slowly covered her one shovel at a time from each man. We said prayers for her soul to rest in peace. Then we made our way back down the hill to the farm.

At the farm, while the men were preparing to leave, Zuber Shala pulled me to one-side.

'I will not be going back with you,' he said in a low voice.

He looked pale and grief stricken. He had gone back to the garage alone and stood for a while in silence with his thoughts. One of the men had given him a photo from the house that he had found of the young girl. The photo of the young girl had been taken recently. Her name and the date of the taken photo was handwritten on the back. She was strikingly beautiful and faced the camera smiling, her whole life ahead of her at the very moment that the photo was taken.

'What do you mean,' I said, trying to keep my voice down. 'You are not going back. What do you plan to do. Stay here,' I asked, incredulously.

'No. I have to go to my studio. I need to paint. I have to paint. The image in my head is torturing me. I have to release it the only way that I know how. That is to paint. I have to go. I must.'

'But your studio is in Pristina. You know that it is not safe to travel there. The Capital is dangerous with ethnic cleansing taking place. It is foolhardy. You can't go.' I said firmly, trying to contain my anger.

Zuber Shala looked at me calmly. 'I will and I must.'

I knew that I could not talk him out of it. Wild horses would not stop him once he had made up his mind to do something. I sighed. 'Okay. But I insist that I go with you. The men can continue the search for other properties, then head back. Agreed.'

I gave him little choice. He knew that I too could not be talked out of it. We were both stubborn as mules.

'Agreed. We are leaving now.'

The studio was on the top floor of a large building, built at the turn of the century. Zuber Shala collected the keys from the caretaker that lived in an apartment on the ground floor, and he assured us that this part of the City remained relatively peaceful.

We climbed the central staircase that led to his apartment and studio. The apartment was simply furnished, with wooden flooring and the walls painted white throughout, with the doors and frames and skirting boards painted in a duck egg blue. The apartment had large windows to the front and back. Overlooking the street below and a courtyard at the back. The studio had skylights that flooded the space with natural light. We had some provisions bought from a store for our stay. I said I would cook a meal and make coffee, while he got to work, as I could see that he was eager to begin.

After selecting a large canvas and getting the paint that he required ready, we stopped to eat. Then he began.

I stood and watched as he painted the canvas with a grey paint that matched that of the tarpaulin. He left it to dry and said that he would begin again in the morning as it was late and the sky was darkening and he would lose the natural light.

I found him in the morning working furiously on the canvas with red paint. He had awoken at first light and had got straight into it. He worked tirelessly, applying the paint with a pallet knife, brushes, working the paint over the canvas with his bare hands. I made him coffee throughout the day and lit his cigarettes as he worked without a break, refusing to eat, just drinking the coffee and smoking cigarette after cigarette. He poured his heart and soul into the painting. Every fibre of his being. When he finished he was exhausted, mentally and physically. He had truly suffered for his art.

He did not ask me what I felt about the painting, not that I had any knowledge about what was good art or bad. I just knew that it was the most powerful piece of art that I have ever seen. He stood back to look at the finished canvas. Then calmly said.

'We can now go back.'

He locked up the apartment and handed the keys back to the caretaker. That evening we travelled back to the fate that awaited us.

I lay on the bed after the driver had gone. And I knew that I had to see the painting by Zuber Shala again after being told the story of the Red Garage Floor.

That night I dreamt of ghostly figures, loud singing and shouting. Gunfire exploding like fireworks. And blood. I felt myself drowning in a sea of red and all along the haunting face of a beautiful girl.

I awoke covered in sweat, the sleeping bag damp where I lay. I was hot but strangely shivering, chilled to the bone, scared and alone. Awaiting my fate.

14

The gunman suddenly burst into the room and he was waving his gun about. To me he looked worse for wear through drinking and at that moment I was quite terrified at what he may do. Alcohol and guns was a dangerous mix and a cocktail that I could do without. Playing it cool was my only option so I sat still on the bed and did breathing exercises that I used before matches to keep me calm and focused. All the way through from the moment that I was thrown into the back of a van to being kept under lock and key I have been grateful that I had worked with my psychologist at the club. That I have been given a lot of coping mechanisms, like breathing and meditation. Learning how to bring yourself into the present. To stop letting your subconscious take over.

'This,' he said, looking at his gun. 'Is a Taurus G3 9mm. Got it boxed brand new.'

He looked like a kid with a new toy. Except it wasn't a toy, it was a handgun and very real.

'Do you know what you are worth, Jack,' he asked.

I looked at him and smiled, because he was smiling at me. Which was good. Stay smiling I thought and maybe when he has had his bit of fun he may go.

'Well,' he said. 'How fucking much. You must have an idea, eh.'

'Not exactly,' I said, giving an honest answer because I didn't know exactly.

The gunman kept his smile. Went and sat on the smoking chair, and as soon as he sat on it, out came his cigarettes. He had to put the gun down on the floor to get his cigarettes out and to light the cigarette. Once it was lit he picked it up again, his new toy and he couldn't bear to be parted from it.

'Looking at me, Jack, would you think, I bet he can't sail. I reckon I am right, eh. Doesn't look the type to be messing about on boats. Be clueless. Well you'd be wrong. I am an excellent sailor. Can handle a boat as easily as sitting here having a smoke. And that is what I want. My very own boat, and not a big yacht, just a boat that I can sail single-handed and not have to worry about anything ever again as I sail away into the sun. My dream. The money to do that, eh. Then gonna find me that place in the sun.'

The gunman sighed.

'Do you know what I am worth, Jack.'

I had not got a clue, or even a guess. 'Don't know.'

He laughed and smoke billowed from his mouth like his head was on fire. 'Well, Jack. I shall tell you. As of this moment, Jack shit.'

And then he was no longer laughing. And it wiped the smile from my face. As he sat for a moment smoking in silence.

For the briefest moment I actually felt sorry for him, almost sad. I could see it in his eyes how much he wanted it, but knew his dream was just that, a dream and not reality. But only for the briefest moment, as he held out his gun and looked straight down the barrel pointing the gun at me. He then pulled out the magazine of the gun to reveal the bullets. He showed them to me. Then pushed the magazine back so it was ready to fire. 'Jack,' he said slowly. 'If they don't pay up I am not walking away and you handed back like nothing happened. You understand that, don't you.'

I understood exactly what he was saying. One or more of those bullets were for me if a ransom was refused.

I just moved my head slowly up and down. A nod was as good as a wink to a blind horse.

There was nothing that I could say or do. Begging for my life seemed pointless. He could not give a fuck and would shoot me without thinking about it. Not bat an eyelid as he pulled the trigger. Shoot me dead as his dream was shot to pieces.

The gunman slowly rose to his feet. 'Glad we got that cleared up, Jack. Gonna go now. Left my drink downstairs. My birthday. Say happy birthday, Jack.'

'Happy birthday.' But I didn't mean it and it came out that way. I wished him a massive heart attack on his birthday right there in front of me. The driver also. Step over their dead bodies and get home to my family.

'You don't sound like you mean it. But then why would you.'

And laughing out loud the gunman left the room. Turned the key in the lock and was still laughing loudly as he walked away. Back to his birthday party. Leaving me on my Jack Jones.

Back in the kitchen the gunman squeezed the finished can of lager in his hand and took aim at the waste bin, like a basketball player sizing up a shot. The can flew through the air and landed in the waste bin. The gunman punched the air, and then pulled the ring on another can of lager from a pack in front of him on the kitchen table.

The driver watched while he poured himself a glass of wine from an opened bottle. Raised his glass to the gunman. 'Happy birthday.'

The gunman grinned and held up his can of lager. 'Cheers, mate.'

'You went to the room. What did you say to him.'

'Nothing much. Just a friendly chat, that's all.'

The driver looked at the handgun on the kitchen table. And looked back to the gunman. 'A friendly chat with a gun in your hand.'

'Yeah, a friendly chat. So what.'

The driver drank some wine then put the glass back down. He sighed. 'We agreed whatever happens we will not harm Jack.'

'The gunman stared hard at the driver. 'You agreed.'

'We agreed,' said the driver, his eyes going cold as he stared back.

The gunman laughed. 'Keep your hair on. We both agreed, okay. Feel better now. End of. My birthday and I never get into any kind of agro on my birthday.'

The driver looked at the new handgun on the table. 'Your birthday present to yourself. Another gun to play with.'

The gunman picked it up. Pointed it away from the driver and looked down the barrel taking aim at the little Yorkie sleeping curled on a blanket. Laughed. Then put the gun back down. 'I offered you my old gun.'

'You know that I will not carry a gun so what use would it be to me. Better you sell it, yes. Help pay for your new gun.'

The gunman grinned. 'That I did, mate. Anyhow. Talking about my birthday. I fancy an Indian tonight.'

The driver pushed himself up from the kitchen table. 'Your birthday, I will cook you something special.'

'Sit back down. My birthday isn't it. And I want an Indian. And my treat, eh. I'll order you a vegetable biryani. I am ordering now …' and the gunman picked up his mobile phone from the table and went onto the deliveroo app.

'Found him outside the police station, sergeant.'

The duty sergeant looked at the young man, a delivery driver for deliveroo, standing in the reception area with a police constable. He looked at the police constable that had walked him into the police station and presented him to the front desk that he was responsible for. 'No one here has ordered a takeaway.'

'No, sergeant. He is here to report about a robbery.'

'Right. Go on, then,' said the duty sergeant to the young man.

The young man put his insulated bag on the floor. 'Well. I was robbed at gunpoint. Not sure that it was a real gun. Looked real enough and I wasn't gonna argue. The man took my helmet and my scooter. He had a small dog under his arm. Telling you, I was scared, the man meant business with his gun stuck in my face. I reported the robbery after it happened.'

'I bet you were scared. Anyway, if you reported it, why are you here,' asked the sergeant. Looking at the police constable, then back to the young man.

The duty sergeant sucked on the end of his Biro. He was craving a cigarette and couldn't wait for his break to light up. The end of the Biro was no substitute for the real thing, but it gave his hands something to do as he held the Biro like a cigarette and continued the pretence of smoking as if it was a burning cigarette on the go.

'I am here because I just delivered an Indian meal. And the man that took the meal from me was the same man that robbed me of my helmet and scooter. Same man, I am telling you. When he robbed me the first thing that I did was look down at his trainers. adidas Sobakov Black. Two-hundred pound trainers. I always checkout the footwear. And then his teeth, they dazzled. Really white teeth. He opened the door and the same trainers. And dazzling teeth. That was my man. The man that robbed me.'

'Do you think that he recognised you, this man.'

'No. He just took the meal. Said it was his birthday. Give me a tenner tip. Ten-pounds. Good tip. And I thought, even though you tipped me a good tip, I'm still going to the police.'

The duty sergeant looked at the young man, took the end of the Biro from his mouth. 'Okay, then. We better get you into the interview room and take some details.'

15

Sergeant Bob Smith picked up his phone as it rang on his desk.

'Thought I should call you, Bob, straight away,' said the duty sergeant. 'A young man that delivers for deliveroo has just delivered an Indian meal. And guess who ordered it.'

'Prince Charles.'

'No, Bob. Not Prince Charles. A young man has just been interviewed over a robbery that he reported. Your team was involved. They had been chasing a suspect with a stolen dog and he robbed the young man at gunpoint and took his helmet and scooter and made his getaway. That same young man had just delivered an Indian, and the person that took the meal was the same person that had robbed him. He swears on it, that it is the same man. And I believe him.'

Sergeant Bob Smith gripped his phone with relief. This could be the lucky break that they had been after. He was sure that the suspect that they had been following was responsible for the spate of dog thefts. And he was armed and although the handgun could be a fake, they would take no chances. They would go full Robocop and request a Firearms Support Unit in case the gun was real. And now thanks to deliveroo they had his whereabouts.

'Fuck me.'

'That is what I said, Bob. Fuck me. And knew that you'd be pleased and want to know straight away.'

'Pleased. I am over the fucking moon. I really appreciate it. Your next drink is on me. Send me over the details by email and meanwhile I will get the team together and go and get the bastard. And thanks again.'

The bucket-sized waste bin overflowed with squashed lager cans and several lay on the floor around it. On the table were empty cartons of Indian food, several unopened cans of lager and a finished bottle of wine and an opened one on the go. And a saucer used as an ashtray overflowing with stubbed-out cigarettes. The kitchen stank of Indian food and cigarettes.

The gunman moved in his chair to lift a bum cheek and farted loudly, adding to the smell. He grinned. 'Excuse my manners.'

The driver blew cigarette smoke towards the ceiling and ignored his crude friend.

The gunman pushed a newspaper towards the driver. 'Go on. Read it again.'

'I have read it.'

'Not aloud. Read it aloud. Go on.'

The driver sighed. Anything to keep him amused on his birthday as he picked up the newspaper and looked again at the headlines on the front page. He put the newspaper down for a moment while he finished his cigarette. He took a last long drag on his cigarette and then stubbed the end into the saucer. He picked the saucer up and emptied it into one of the empty curry cartons. Then picked up the newspaper and read aloud to the gunman just to please him.

'Police frustration over the missing footballer, Jack Jones. A police spokesperson said there was increasing frustration over the disappearance of the footballer. They are following possible sightings by members of the public that have been from Land's End to John o' Groats. And sightings in Europe and beyond. They have officers working around the clock on the case and are leaving no stone unturned but at the moment they are drawing a blank. All they have at this moment in time is one simple fact. He left his house then simply vanished …'

The gunman laughed aloud. 'Too right he vanished. What did I say at the time. It was our lucky day. He just walked out right in front of us and not a soul around. Not a single living person witnessed the kidnapping. Jack Jones went in a puff of smoke …' and the gunman puffed out a cloud of cigarette smoke. He grinned from ear to ear, stupidly pleased at the result.

'What a result, eh. And I'll tell you what, mate. They will never find him.'

The driver raised his glass to their success. 'We will make contact tomorrow and end this. We get our money and then get on with our new lives. Jack Jones can go back to his family.'

'Too right,' as the gunman raised his can of lager and drank to their new lives that awaited them.

And the Yorkshire Terrier suddenly started to bark excitedly, running around the kitchen as it barked loudly.

The gunman got to his feet and went to the window to see what was outside that was making the dog go loopy. He pulled back from the window and shouted to the driver.

'Fucking swarming with police …' and he looked at his gun on the kitchen table. 'They ain't having Jack …'

The driver got the handgun first.

'Give me the fucking gun …' shouted the gunman, his eyes blazing with anger.

This was met by a steely gaze. 'We agreed to not harm Jack …' and the driver chucked the handgun and it clattered to the floor in the corner of the kitchen as the Firearms Support Unit burst in after smashing their way into the property.

The gunman and the driver were quickly overpowered and held face down on the floor. Cuffed then led away. The Firearms Support Unit stood down once their job was done and every room in the property had been cleared. They handed over the crime scene to the dognapping team that would begin the search of the property. Items like the handgun and cash put into forensic bags. Along with burner phones and the Polaroid camera. And the hunt for stolen dogs.

An officer from the dognapping team came outside looking for his sergeant, who had left the property earlier with the two arrested people to oversee them taken into custody and would be interviewed by him at an appropriate time. As the van pulled away with the two prisoners he got out his cigarettes. He was having a smoke by his car as the officer approached. And the night sky darkened as clouds covered the moon, and the tip of his cigarette glowed red.

'Is everything going okay with the search.'

'Yes, sergeant. And you won't believe it when I tell you who we found. Honestly, sergeant. Just unbelievable.'

Sergeant Bob Smith took a long pull on his cigarette. Exhaled. 'Hopefully you'll tell me that you have found Cruella de Vil and 101 stolen Dalmatians.'

'Better than that, sergeant.'

'What can be better than that. We came looking for dogs. Stolen dogs that we can reunite with their owners. All we have so far is a Yorkshire Terrier.'

The officer smiled. 'Do you mind if I have a quick smoke, sergeant. I think I need one.'

'Be my guest.' Sergeant Bob Smith waited while the officer got a cigarette in his mouth and lit.

The officer took a satisfied long pull before slowly exhaling the smoke away from his sergeant.

'Well,' said Sergeant Bob Smith. 'I am waiting for you to tell me who you found. We have two people so far, are you telling me there is a third person that was hiding.'

'Not hiding, sergeant. Being held. Held against his will, the missing Jack Jones. We found a locked room upstairs. Broke it down and went in. Inside the room was Jack Jones.'

Sergeant Bob Smith looked taken-aback. Like he could not quite believe his ears. 'Jack

Jones. What. The Jack Jones. Jack Jones the missing footballer.'

The officer laughed in response. 'Yes, sergeant. As I live and breathe. We have found him. Jack Jones had been bundled into the back of a van as he left his house and brought here. Been here all this time.'

Sergeant Bob Smith whistled long and loud. Then looked at the officer. 'Fuck me.'

The officer grinned. 'That is what I said, sergeant, when I realised who it was. Fuck me.'

Sergeant Bob Smith finished his cigarette and dropped the remains to the ground. He felt in a bit of a daze with the unexpected news. They had come here looking for stolen dogs and to arrest whoever was responsible. Came fully-prepared. But no shootouts. No heroics. Two culprits taken away. And he would have been happy just to find some missing dogs to reunite with their owners. But now they had found the missing Jack Jones. What a turn up for the books. deliveroo had delivered Jack Jones to them. You couldn't make it up.

'Is he okay.'

The officer took a long drag on his cigarette, blew the smoke skyward. 'Sound, sergeant. Obviously he was scared witless when the door was broken down and the firearms unit went in dressed in full gear and pointed guns.

But once the shock of that was over and he realised who we were he was mightily pleased that for him it was now all over. His kidnapping has come to an end. He can get back to his family. One of our team is looking after him. And we have requested a medic to check him over. But like I say, he seems pretty sound.'

'Good,' said Sergeant Bob Smith. Still trying to absorb the news.

The officer finished his cigarette, dropped the end and crushed it under his shoe. 'Did say, sergeant, it was just unbelievable. To think, we have police looking far and wide for the football star and we find him here when we came looking for stolen dogs. Unbelievable. And what makes it so special for me is that I follow Fulham. They are my team and I am a season ticket holder. And there was Jack Jones alive and well. Unbelievable, sergeant. No other word for it.'

Sergeant Bob Smith needed another cigarette. He lit it with his lighter and took a long pull. Slowly exhaled while the events of the evening sank in. The officer was right. It was unbelievable and there was no other word for it. 'I bet you told him to stay at Fulham and not sign for another club.'

The officer laughed. 'No, sergeant, I didn't. But if he does leave I wish him well.'

Sergeant Bob Smith exhaled slowly into the night sky and watched as the smoke drifted upwards and looked for a moment at the white glow of the full moon as the clouds parted like curtains and it was back on show. He looked back at the officer. 'We all wish him well. As soon as we can, let's get him back to his family.'

16

Once the media-circus had died down and my life was back to normal I wanted to go back and see the painting by Zuber Shala again. I had to see it as I would see it now and not when I first saw it and dismissed it as not much to look at and just a canvas of red paint that anyone could have done and really not meaning much, to me at least. I had to see the painting to bring closure.

So I stood in front of the canvas and looked at it with fresh eyes and knew the story behind it. I could now see the pain and suffering in every layer of red paint that had been applied and the meaning behind the grey area in the corner. I could now see a tarpaulin covering a beautiful young girl that was too terrified to leave the safety of her hiding place. The canvas in front of me was as powerful as the painting by Picasso, Guernica, to the horrors of war.

I stood in utter silence as tears rolled down my face and Jill squeezed my hand. I just stood there staring at the canvas as I now realised how meaningful and powerful art could be.

We came outside Jill and I to summer sunshine, not a cloud in the sky. Wyn had waited outside with our gorgeous daughter. I picked her up and smothered her with kisses then handed her over to Jill. Then bent down and scooped up Yorkie, my little soul mate. Laughed as he licked my face before putting him back down on the ground. I fancied a beer. The pub was a short walk away.

'Fancy a beer,' I said to Jill.

Jill laughed. 'Yeah, why not.'

Printed in Great Britain
by Amazon